I scanned the bleachers for someone to go sit with. Anyone.

Then my heart jumped.

Graham was sitting in the next section, leaning back, propped up with his elbows on the bench behind him. His jeans were faded, his sneakers were hashed, and he was wearing a Red Sox cap backward and a red sweat-shirt. It was the first time I'd seen him in anything but shorts and cleats.

As I watched, he turned his head and looked right at me. Then he grinned.

Stephie Davis

The Boyfriend Game

HARPER TEEN
AN IMPRINT OF HARPERCOLLINSPUBLISHERS

HarperTeen is an imprint of HarperCollins Publishers.

The Boyfriend Game
Copyright © 2009 by Stephanie Rowe
All rights reserved. Printed in the United States of America.
No part of this book may be used or reproduced in any man-
ner whatsoever without written permission except in the case
of brief quotations embodied in critical articles and reviews.
For information address HarperCollins Children's Books,
a division of HarperCollins Publishers, 1350 Avenue of the
Americas, New York, NY 10019.
www.harperteen.com

Library of Congress Catalog Card Number: 2006934361
ISBN 978-0-06-114310-6

First Edition

To all the girls who have found the joy in sports, sweating, and accomplishing physical feats they never thought they were capable of. Never give up!

1

The afternoon sun was beating down on my shoulders as I watched an evil leer light up the face of my best friend, Sara Myers. Her long legs were like sticks below her shorts, and there was the faintest gleam of sweat over the upturned nose that she swore was her only decent feature. "Just try and stop me, Trisha," she taunted, her dark curls bouncing with each step.

"Just try and get by me," I shot back, grinning as she got closer. It might be just a routine one-on-one drill on a Thursday afternoon of JV soccer practice, but it was always a lot more than that when I was going one-on-one with Sara.

Sara was better than me at soccer. And she didn't even try. I busted my butt. And she was still better. Totally bugged me.

But she hated the fact that over the summer, I'd gotten a real figure and she was still as skinny as ever, so we were even. Especially since we'd totally make the trade if we could. She'd take all the attention I got from guys in a heartbeat, and I'd give that up in a minute if I could have her soccer skills. Actually, I'd give it up in a minute for free, if I could. Only six weeks into my freshman year of high school and already I was tired of the boys treating me differently than they used to. Hello? What was wrong with noticing I played good defense, instead of commenting on how my shirt fit?

Sara's smile faded into concentration, and I focused on every angle of her body, trying to anticipate what move she'd pull to try to get past me. My muscles tensed, and I felt the zip of adrenaline that I loved, the sensation of power that had me running for the soccer field every afternoon, totally pumped to sweat and yell and forget about all the baggage of my day at school. On the soccer field, it wasn't about boys and girls or how I looked. It was about how good you were. It was my favorite place to be.

"Hey, Trisha! Looking good out there!"

Sara sucked in her breath, and I scowled at the sound

of Kirk Nichols' obnoxious voice, not even bothering to glance at the sidelines where I knew he'd be standing with his loyal shadow, Ross Crane. Probably wearing Nike sunglasses, baseball hats, and faded jeans, like they always did, knowing just how to dress to look good.

Well, they *were* cute, but they were also idiots, so I shut them out and concentrated on Sara. Her gaze flicked toward Kirk, and I grinned. Oh, she was so busted. *Keep yelling, Kirk.* One little distraction was more than enough for me to take her out.

"Trisha! Hey, Trisha Perkins! You gonna come to Pop's tonight with me, or what?" Kirk shouted.

Sara scowled at me. I bit my lip and quickly adjusted to her sudden increase in intensity. *Great.* So now she was going to take it out on me that Kirk was yelling my name and not hers. Classic Kirk. Always screwing up my life.

"Sara! Tell her she has to come!" Kirk shouted.

Sara's cheeks turned pink and she shot a quick look in his direction. I lunged forward to take advantage of the distraction, my cleats grabbing the turf as I plucked the ball from between her feet. She spun around, and I dodged her, making a snarky face at Kirk, who was yelling something about how he liked my new haircut. He should be shouting about my great steal, not making some stupid comment about my *hair*. So typical of Kirk, and of guys in general. I turned my head to glare at him . . . and noticed a guy standing next to him and Ross.

The guy was taller than them, had short dark hair, and was wearing soccer cleats. And shorts that showed off his oh-so-muscular soccer legs. He was holding a soccer ball against his hip, his arm hanging loosely over it. Who the heck was he?

Before I knew it, Sara was next to me, her feet were on the ball, then I went flying. I threw up my arms as I went skidding on my left hip and wound up in a face-plant in the grass. Sara crowed in victory and I rolled to a sitting position, spitting grass out of my mouth.

Kirk and Ross howled with laughter, and I immediately glanced over to them. To the guy.

Who was gone.

I made a quick scan of the fields, but I didn't see him anymore. Where'd he go?

My other best friend, Beth Stevenson, walked up and peered down at me. She was wearing cleats and a tee shirt like I was, but she was still clean. No sweat and no dirt. Not that it was a surprise. She only played JV soccer to hang out with us. I played to play. Sara played . . . well . . . I was never quite sure with Sara.

"You almost had her," Beth said.

I sighed. "I know." It was always *almost* when it came to beating Sara at soccer.

Beth held out her hand and pulled me up. "I mean, you did have her, and then you let her come back and get you. What was up with that?"

As if I were going to tell her that I'd let a boy distract me. Ha! That was a Sara move, not something I would do. Actually, it was totally embarrassing. So I shrugged. "I felt bad for her. Didn't want to show her up with Kirk watching."

Beth snorted. "Yeah, right. You have no mercy on the soccer field."

"You say that like it's a bad thing." My thigh was burning big-time, so I hiked up my shorts and inspected the raspberry that started up by my hip and went halfway down my thigh. It was already bright red. I grinned, loving the badge of honor it gave me. Despite what Kirk might think, there was so much more to me than what I looked like. I was a warrior! "There goes my plan to wear a miniskirt tomorrow," I joked.

Kirk and Ross yelled and whistled, so I pulled my shorts back down to cover my leg, my cheeks suddenly hot. Guys were so annoying!

Beth raised both her eyebrows. They were carefully shaped to augment her bright blue eyes, courtesy of a makeover by Sara last weekend that had ended up with all of us sporting highlights and new haircuts. Not that you could tell with me, except for the fact that some of the layers weren't staying in my ponytail very well. Well, you could see the auburn highlights in the darker brown of my natural hair color, but that was it.

"You've never owned a skirt in your life," Beth said. "Of any kind."

I grinned. I definitely wasn't a skirt girl. Especially this year, since guys like Kirk had started bugging me. Nothing like getting a figure over the summer to change the way guys acted around you, I guess. From normal human beings to loud, annoying, and general pests.

I was sticking with jeans, thanks.

"Nice raspberry." Sara flounced toward us, shooting a flirtatious grin in the direction of the sidelines. "Totally uncool to take advantage of me when Kirk distracted me. If I hadn't beaten you in the end, I'd make you kiss my toes." A reference to when we were little and dorky, and we used to make the other one actually kiss our toes when we made up from a fight, or after one of us did something mean to the other.

"There would have been no toe kissing," I shot back. "It's your own fault for not paying attention."

Sara was wearing a fitted tee shirt and spandex shorts and was having a successful trial with her new water-proof makeup. She was tall, thin, and had thick curly hair—everything that Beth didn't, with her short, stockier figure. But Beth was blond, and I knew Sara would kill for Beth's straight, golden locks.

They were both totally cute and into the guys. I mean, Sara had dropped her notebook last week and I'd seen that she'd written Kirk's name all over the inside cover, not that she'd ever admit it out loud. And Beth was right there with her in checking the guys out. They both spent ten minutes doing their makeup before practice, in hopes of getting dorks like Kirk to yell at them.

Whatever.

Coach Merrill blew her whistle. "I have an announcement to make."

I noticed Kirk and Ross standing in the distance. Kirk was mouthing something to me and pointing to his hip, where I'd burned mine in the grass. I felt Sara looking at me, so I folded my arms and turned toward Coach Merrill and away from Kirk.

"Every season at the end of October, I pick two girls from JV to move up to varsity for the rest of the season," Coach Merrill said. "Two weeks from this Friday, we'll be having tryouts with the varsity practice. The top five girls on JV will be invited to that practice, and two will move up."

No way! I had no idea! *Varsity.* How awesome would

that be? My heart started racing. I inched closer so I wouldn't miss any of the details.

"So, I wanted to announce the five short-listed players, so you can tell me if you're interested in being considered."

I stole a glance at Sara. She was better than I was, but she didn't work nearly as hard. Would Coach take that into account? Five spots weren't very many when there were over forty girls on the squad.

Sara was watching Kirk and Ross, not paying any attention to Coach. A little part of me hoped Coach noticed. I mean, I *didn't* want Coach to notice, because Sara was my friend and she deserved to be on varsity, but she didn't want a spot on varsity. Not like I did. So maybe I sort of hoped Coach would call her on it.

"The players I'm considering are Kathleen Hoffman . . ."

"She's the best player on our team," Beth whispered.

I shushed her with my hand, holding my breath.

"Heidi Maxwell . . ."

"Oh, I didn't think of her. She's great at defense," Beth said.

"Ssh!"

"Vicky Conant . . ."

Sara leaned over. "Beth, I think Ross is checking you out."

Beth smacked Sara on the arm. "No way! Really?" She turned bright red and immediately turned her back on the boys. "Trisha, you look at them and tell me if she's lying."

"Shut up!" I stepped away from them, straining to listen as the other girls on the team started whispering.

"Sara Myers . . ."

I bit my lip against the sudden swell of jealousy as I heard Beth squeal behind me. Great. I was *so* happy for Sara.

"And Trisha Perkins."

Yes!

Beth threw her arms around me. "Trisha! That's so awesome! You guys are too cool!"

Coach said something about practice being over for the day, but I didn't hear her. My heart was pounding too loudly and Beth was squealing in my ear. She had both me and Sara in a headlock and it took less than a minute for the three of us to end up in a pile on the grass. I was still laughing and trying to get untangled when the sun was blocked and a shadow fell over us.

Sara got quiet as Kirk leaned over us. "Competition among friends," he teased. "Who's going to win? Trish or Sara? Are we going to have a girl fight?"

I rolled my eyes. "Shut up."

See? This is why I avoided Kirk. Total idiot. Hello?

Where were the congratulations? The appreciation for being picked for the short list? He had no clue about what was important.

"You wish, Kirk." Sara giggled. "But we'll be sure to call you if we do."

Beth and I exchanged a groan, then Kirk grabbed my hand and tugged me to my feet before I could jerk away from him. "How about going to Pop's for a little celebration, Trisha? A little dancing, maybe?" His gaze flicked to my hair. "A quick shower and a change of clothes and you'll be smoking."

I yanked my hand out of his grip. "No, thanks." Pop's was the local hangout for the kids at our high school. They served great pizza, had free refills on soda, and owned a sweet jukebox stocked with all the best tunes, including the newest JamieX CD. I'd been so psyched to start going there once we were freshmen, but lately it totally bummed me out. It was all about guys being loud and obnoxious and checking out the girls, and girls worrying about their hair and their makeup and giggling at the guys. I had no interest in hanging out while everyone flirted with one another. Especially Kirk. Instead, I flaunted the grass stain on my shirt and said, "I'm going to practice some more."

"Practice?" Kirk laughed. "Are you kidding? It's

Thursday night. Time to party."

Sara fluffed her hair and smiled at him. "I'll go to Pop's with you. Trisha might be antisocial, but I'm not."

I frowned at her remark. She hadn't made comments like that before this fall, when Kirk had started noticing me. "I take soccer seriously. That's a good thing."

"Unless it gets in the way of fun," Sara said. "Come on, Beth. Let's go shower." She gave Kirk a special smile. "We'll be ready in twenty minutes. Can you wait?"

"Sure." He took another look at me, then headed off toward the gym with Ross in tow.

I leveled a look at Sara. "I'm not fun?"

"If you pick soccer over hanging out with Kirk at Pop's, yeah."

I folded my arms, a sudden hope flaring in my chest. "So, does that mean you're going to turn down Coach for the varsity thing?"

She glanced at Kirk's receding back, then met my gaze. "Do you want me to?"

"Ha. Of course not." But even as I said the words, I realized I was sort of lying. If Sara dropped out, I had a much better chance at making varsity. I was probably tied with Heidi as the third best on the team, behind Sara and Kathleen. But I wanted Sara on there with me. Together.

But if it came down to her or me . . . No. She was my

friend. I wanted her to get it too. I swallowed hard and managed a smile. "Why don't you stay and practice with me? I could really use your help to bone up on my skills in the next two weeks."

She cocked her head, actually considering it, then Kirk ruined it.

"Hey, Trisha!" Kirk yelled, and Sara's mouth tightened. "I'll save you a seat in case you change your mind. You know you can't resist me forever!"

Sara hesitated. "I'm going for varsity, but I'm not going to miss out on fun by staying late to practice. I'm going with Kirk and Ross." Then she turned away and broke into a jog to run after the guys.

Beth hugged me. "Congrats again, Trish. I'm so psyched for you. I know you can make it."

Yeah, maybe. But it was going to be a lot harder if I had to practice by myself. I couldn't help but watch as Sara caught up to the boys. I didn't want them going out without me. I mean, I didn't want to *go*, but I wanted them to stay with me. All girls, like it used to be. "Do you want to stay and practice with me?"

Beth wrinkled her nose. "Sorry, but more than an hour of soccer a day gives me hives. You sure you don't want to come to Pop's?"

I kicked my toe in the dirt. "Yeah. Are you sure you

don't want to stay here?"

"Totally sure. Have fun." She patted my shoulder and ran off, hollering at Sara to wait up. I watched as she caught up, shooting a shy glance at Ross before settling in next to Sara. I could hear their laughter all the way across the field.

I sighed and started to get majorly depressed, then suddenly realized that the varsity girls were jogging toward me on their way to take over our field for practice. Oh, *cool*.

I forgot all about my friends and Kirk as I watched the varsity players start drilling. For a few minutes, I was in awe of their footwork and their ball-handling skills. They were joking around and having fun, but they were totally serious too. I'd miss JV, but this was so my world. I *belonged*.

Then I realized how much better they were than I was.

How much I needed to improve to have a chance with them.

Shoot. I didn't belong. Not yet. Not by a long shot.

Even *Sara* needed to get better.

And she wasn't practicing, was she? I should run to the gym and tell her.

I should.

But I didn't. She'd made her choice, right? Instead, I

snagged a ball and headed over to the smaller practice field behind the equipment shed. I heard Sara screech and I jerked my gaze to the gym in time to see her and Beth duck inside, giggling about something.

My stomach curled up in a little knot, but I ground my teeth and spun back toward the field. I loved soccer. I wanted varsity. Giving up a little time with my friends rotted, but it was worth it. They didn't get me, not this part of me. The part of me that loved to have grass stains on my shorts and sweat rolling down my temples. The part that loved being out there with the ball, in a world where nothing mattered except how you played.

I broke into a jog, dribbling the ball in front of me, a sense of rightness settling over me as my muscles started to work. No Kirk around to judge me and make me feel stupid for not caring about my hair. No boys to make dumb comments about girl fights instead of appreciating that a girl could be athletic . . .

I rounded the corner and saw the guy I'd noticed during practice. I immediately tripped on my soccer ball and went down. I popped back up, watching as he dribbled two balls through an obstacle course of cones.

His head was down and his body loose. He had the great build that all soccer players have, with strong legs and fit upper bodies. His hair was dark and stuck to his head. Unlike Kirk-the-idiot, he'd been sweating. And he was good too. Why hadn't I seen him before? I knew everyone who played soccer.

Not that it mattered. It wasn't like I was going to talk to him.

I picked up my ball and started to turn away to find somewhere else to practice, when he lifted his head and looked right at me.

And I totally forgot what I'd been about to do.

2

He stopped drilling, flicked one of the balls up with his toe, then bounced it off his knee, then flipped his foot behind him and caught the ball off his heel. Hackey sack for soccer players, and he was good.

He bounced the ball high off his thigh, let it land on his forehead, then headed it straight up in the air, then did it again, dribbling off his forehead, arms out for balance, feet moving quickly to stay under the ball.

Okay, he was *really* good.

And showing off. Typical guy. Why couldn't guys just be normal?

I rolled my eyes and started to turn away, then saw

him head the ball at me.

Reacting instinctively, I spun back toward him and blocked it with my foot. He grinned and nailed the second ball at me. I headed it back toward him and he trapped it with his right foot. He flipped the ball up at me again with his toe and I caught it as he walked up. "Nice reactions," he said.

No comment about my hair or my looks? That alone was almost enough to redeem him from showing off with the hackey sack moves. "Thanks."

"What's up?" He raised his brows in question, and I noticed his eyes. Greenish brown. Intense. Not like Kirk's, which were always shifting and checking me out and stuff. This guy was simply waiting for an answer. Like he actually wanted to know what I had to say.

I relaxed a little bit. "Soccer." Like anything else mattered, right? He was out here practicing. He might actually understand where I was coming from.

He nodded. "Me too. I'm Graham Fordham, just transferred here a couple weeks ago. You are . . . ?" There were trickles of sweat dripping down the sides of his face. He didn't smell bad, though. He just had the scent of sports. Of athletics. It was real, not like Kirk's cologne or whatever he used. I liked it. I mean, I didn't *like* it, like it. It just made me feel comfortable.

So I grinned. "Trisha."

He used his toe to tug my ball out from under my foot and I let him. "So, what are you doing on the fields at this hour?" he asked.

"Trying to find a place to practice. You?"

He started in on the hackey sack thing again, and this time I realized that he was paying more attention to the ball than to me. Maybe he wasn't showing off. Maybe he was just doing it because he liked to do it.

Huh. If I could do that, I'd probably do it a lot too.

"Same here," he said. "I need to beat out Tim Hamilton for center forward, so I'm taking a little extra practice." He bounced the ball off his right knee, then his left, then right, then left. . . . "You any good?"

"I can't do *that*," I blurted out.

He grinned, showing a dimple, his gaze flicking briefly to me before focusing on the ball again. "So, that's why you're practicing? Because you're terrible?"

I couldn't help but laugh. "No, I'm not terrible. Why? Are you terrible?"

"Never." He caught the ball and eyed me. "You staying around for a while?"

"'Til it's dark."

"You want to drill, or what?"

A flash of nervousness ran through me. I swallowed, suddenly very aware that he was a guy. Was this his way of making a move on me? Yeah, not interested. "Um, I kinda . . . was going to do some on my own."

He shrugged. "Suit yourself."

Then he turned, dropped the ball, and dribbled away. Instantly, I felt a stab of regret as I watched him maneuver the cones. He'd been totally normal with me, and he was way better than I was. It would have been awesome to drill with him. Awesome because it would help my game, and that's why I was here.

He peered back over his shoulder at me. "You coming?"

I hesitated.

"Afraid you can't keep up with me?" He stopped and started doing the hackey sack thing again.

I smiled. "No way."

"Don't believe you."

I thought of the girls on varsity practicing around the corner and of Sara and Beth off with Kirk, leaving me behind. This kind of practice was exactly what I needed, and he hadn't seemed to even notice I was a girl.

"Well?"

I can handle this. "Fine." I dropped my ball to the field, then dribbled toward him. "I'm in."

He flashed me a grin and then spun back toward the cones. "Follow me."

Five minutes later, he'd reset the cones so there were two lines. One had about twice as many cones as the other, but it was the same setup. He pointed to the one with more cones. "That's my course. We'll start at the same time and race through it. To the end and back. Loser has to run a lap."

I bit back a complaint about the fact he had more cones than I did. If he wanted to give himself a handicap, I'd make him pay. "Fine."

"If you knock down a cone, ten push-ups."

I chuckled. My adrenaline kicked in. "Be prepared to run a lap."

He laughed back. "You'd *better* beat me. You have half the cones I do."

"Oh, I will."

"Let's see it, then." He took his ball and lined up behind the start line he'd set up.

I moved next to him, my muscles relaxed and my mind focused. He was so going down. Guys didn't take girls seriously on the sports field, and he was going to learn he'd made a mistake.

"You call it," he said.

I nodded and took my stance. "Ready."

He set his gaze on the cones.

"Set."

We both tensed.

"Go!"

I took off, burning through the cones, listening to him breathing heavily right beside me. I pressed harder, determined to leave him behind, but he didn't go away. *Come on, Trisha!* The cones blurred past my feet, and I hit the end, spun around the cone, and headed back, digging in as hard as I could, even as I was aware of him pulling ahead of me.

My quads were screaming, but I pushed even more and blew through the last six cones, giving a whoop as I crossed the finish line. He was already done, his chest heaving and a big grin on his face. "Not bad," he said.

"You beat me." I bent over, trying to catch my breath.

He gave a snort of amusement. "If it bugs you, beat me next time."

"Oh, I will. Just give me a second." I was pretty sure I'd never run that hard before in my life. And it *rocked*. He hadn't taken it easy on me, and I loved that. And as soon as the ground stopped spinning, I'd kick his butt.

Then I remembered to check my cones. All standing.

But two of his were down. I shot him a look and he glanced at his course. A flicker of surprise crossed his face, and I felt a smug sense of satisfaction. He'd been concentrating so hard on beating me that he'd messed up. I had a feeling he didn't do that much. "Drop and give me twenty, big guy."

"You still owe me a lap," he grumbled, even as he dropped to the turf and started pumping. "Count 'em."

For a second, I forgot to count as I watched his arms flex with each push-up. His triceps were glistening with sweat, and the muscles were corded under his skin.

He shot me a look. "Six," he prompted.

"Right. Sorry. I was gloating." Then I realized what he'd said. "Nice try, Graham. Try two."

He chuckled. "No mercy." But there was a respect in his voice that made me feel good.

"Like you're going to let me skip my lap."

I was glad when he grunted his refusal. "Not a chance."

"Didn't think so." I sat back on my heels and counted him down, already working on a strategy for my second trip through the cones. Graham was pushing me, and I was challenging him, and it was awesome. He was intense and he was funny, and he took me seriously.

He treated me like one of the guys, and it was the best feeling ever.

None of that girl/guy stuff. Just sweat and sports and competition. Exactly how I wanted it.

An hour and a half later, it was so dark I could barely see the ball, but I wasn't about to call it.

Neither was Graham.

I'd never practiced with someone who was as intense as I was, and it made me try even harder. He'd even set up the drills so it didn't matter that he was a better player. He was still working as hard as I was. I'd done more laps than him, but he'd had to do three. And we'd both done so many push-ups that I was pretty sure I wouldn't be able to lift my toothbrush by the time I got home.

Even my legs were trembling, but I wasn't about to admit it. Not with Graham treating me like a real athlete instead of a pretty ditz or something.

I eyed him as I approached him for a little one-on-one, then faked to the left and split right, then tripped. It was too dark to see. I yelped as I landed on the ball, the leather smacking me like a gut punch.

I groaned and rolled onto my back, letting my arms flop out to my sides. "Ow."

Graham bent over me. "You okay?"

"Yeah." I struggled to sit up, not wanting to be a wimp, but I was so tired, all I wanted to do was lie there in the grass.

"Want a hand?" He held out his hand, and for a minute I hesitated. Was he trying to make a move?

"Come on, klutz. Off your butt."

I grinned and grabbed Graham's outstretched hand and let him pull me to my feet. "Thanks."

"No problem." He flipped the ball into his hands with his toe. "Call it a night?"

I didn't want to, but I knew it was too dark. And I was totally beat. I sighed. "Yeah, I guess we should."

"Aren't you tired?" He scooped the other ball up and tossed me one.

"Not at all," I lied. "You?" I rested the ball on my hip and we walked back toward the equipment shed. Just us. In the dark. Alone. With a boy. I cleared my throat and peeked at him, but he was bouncing the ball off alternating knees with each step. I shook my head. Like I had to worry about anything with him. He was as single-minded as I was when it came to soccer.

"Not tired," Graham said. He still wasn't looking at me. "You stay late much? I've never seen you out here before."

"Actually, this is my first time. Coach told me that she was considering bumping me up to varsity in two weeks, so I decided to stay late and do extra practice."

"Really?" He caught the ball and started tossing it from hand to hand as he walked. "Sweet."

I felt a swell of pride at his tone. He *got* it. "Yeah, I'd be stoked to make varsity. I'm going to practice every day 'til she picks." Man, I would love to practice with Graham again. I'd never been pushed as hard as I'd been tonight, and he'd given me some great tips. A few more sessions with him, and I'd be better than Sara. Well, as good, at least.

We neared the building, the small floodlight lighting up his face. The shadows made his cheekbones prominent and his jaw look really angular. Kind of strong. I suddenly felt intimidated and realized there was no way I'd ask him to practice again. He was on the varsity boys team. A million times better than me. No way was I going to be dumb enough to invite myself into his practice sessions. "So, well, thanks for tonight. It was . . ." Was what? Awesome? Hard as heck and the best night of my life? ". . . fun." Yeah, Trisha the lame-o.

"Yeah, it was good. It's good to have some competition." He caught the ball and gave me a thoughtful look. Not checking me out, not plotting, just normal. "You going to be out here again?"

I eyed him, trying to figure out what he was asking. "I won't get in your way."

He laughed softly. "I meant, do you want to practice again? It helps me to have someone to go against."

Oh, *wow*. He wanted to practice again? With me? I almost shouted my excitement, and then thought of how manic Sara got around guys. I didn't want to be like that, didn't want to make Graham suddenly start thinking of me as a girl, so I gave a casual shrug. "Yeah, that'd be all right."

He tugged open the door and held it for me. "Same time, then?"

"Works for me." I slipped past him, then tossed the ball in the corner.

Graham added his to the pile, then we walked out. He locked the door behind us, and we headed toward the gym.

We were about halfway to the gym when Graham spoke. "So, how come you're not at Pop's? I thought that's where everyone went after school."

"Not everyone." I thought of Sara and Beth there without me, and scowled.

He nodded. "Yeah, I know what you mean. The guys on the team head over there to check out the girls. I'd rather play soccer."

"Really?" I jerked my gaze to his face to see if he was making fun of me. He looked totally serious, and my heart soared. "That's how I feel! My friends just go to hang out with the guys, and everyone acts stupid. I'd so much rather be out here."

Graham laughed again, a low sound that rolled through my bones. "They can't be as dumb as my teammates are. It's like they lose their brains around girls."

"What's up with that?" It was such a relief to talk to someone who thought like I did. I reached the gym door first and I hauled it open.

He reached over my head and grabbed the edge. "Who knows? I can't imagine choosing a girl over sports."

"I know what you mean!" I ducked under his arm and caught another whiff of his scent. It was all guy, with an undercurrent of soap or something. I liked it. Not that I *liked* it . . . okay, fine, I sort of *liked* it. So what? That didn't mean I was going to turn into Sara. I appreciated him as an athlete, and a guy who treated me like an equal. That was it. I took another quick inhale before I moved out of sniffing range. "I'd pick soccer over the scene at Pop's any day."

"I hear you." He let the door shut behind us. "So, I guess that means I'll see you tomorrow?"

I shoved my sweaty bangs off my face and grinned up at him. "Oh, I don't know. I'm thinking I might go to Pop's instead. . . ."

He laughed. "Yeah, right." He jumped down the four steps leading to the boys' locker room, then saluted me. "See ya around, Trisha." Then he shoved open the door to the locker room and disappeared.

I ran all the way down the hall, dancing with excitement. Not only did I have a practice partner, but he felt the same way as I did about our friends and the dating scene.

Graham Fordham was just like me.

Forget Pop's. Forget dating. With him, I didn't have to worry about any of that intimidating guy/girl stuff. I could even make fun of it and he didn't think I was a freak. Plus, I was going to seriously improve my soccer if I kept practicing with him, and that was what really mattered.

I was *so* going to call my dad tonight and tell him about my chance at varsity, and how I was putting in extra practice time.

I slammed my hip into the locker room door and shoved it open, feeling truly happy for the first time in months.

3

Friday night, I found myself sitting between Beth and Sara at the football game, listening to them detail their night at Pop's with Kirk and Ross.

"So, then, Kirk goes up there, and he does karaoke to this Britney Spears song," Sara said. "He was doing all her little dance moves and—" She dissolved into laughter.

"He was actually a really good dancer," Beth said. "But his falsetto was awful! It was too funny! You totally missed out."

I managed a grin. It did sound like it had been fun.

Kirk making a jerk of himself would always be a bonus. Maybe I should have gone. "Yeah, well, I was practicing and I met this—"

Sara elbowed Beth. "It would have been more fun if you and Ross had gone up there. You should have asked him to sing with you."

Beth's cheeks turned red. "No way! He was totally not going up there, and I wasn't going to make an idiot of myself by asking him. You totally lie that he likes me. He barely even looked at me the whole night!"

"Because he's intimidated by your beauty, of course." Sara smirked at me. "Tell her, Trisha. Tell her that Ross likes her, but he's too shy and she's going to have to make the first move."

I wrinkled my nose. "I have no idea if Ross likes you."

"See? He doesn't." Beth folded her arms over her chest and stuck out her jaw. "Don't get me all excited like that, Sara, or I swear I'll tell Kirk that you wrote his name all over the inside of your notebook."

Sara paled and jerked a sharp glance in my direction. As if I didn't already know! "Kirk was checking the door for you all night," she said, almost managing to sound like she didn't care. "Beth, how many times did he ask if Trisha was coming?"

"Like, a zillion," Beth said. "He was sitting next to

the seat we were saving for you and he wouldn't let anyone sit there."

The thought of Kirk waiting for me ended all regret I had at missing out. "What's his problem? Why won't he stop bugging me?"

"Because he likes you, duh," Sara said. "What's *your* problem? Why won't you give him a chance?"

"Totally." Beth sighed and propped her feet up on the empty bleacher in front of us. "You're so lucky. Guys adore you, and you don't even appreciate it."

"Yeah," Sara sighed. "If I had half your chest, my life would be so much better."

I snorted. "Get real. The only reason Kirk likes me is because I don't like him."

"No way," Sara said. "You're *hot*."

I felt my cheeks heat up like they always did when she started talking like that. "Shut up."

Sara leaned on her elbow, twisting around to look at me. "Seriously, do you like him or not? I mean, he seems to think you're playing hard to get."

I rolled my eyes and took a bite of my hot dog. Some questions simply didn't deserve an answer.

Sara bit her lower lip and looked at Beth. I eyed them, realizing they were hatching some plan. I swallowed too soon, choked, and started coughing.

"Smooth move, Trisha," Kirk hollered from down below. "You want me to give you some lessons on how to eat?"

I quickly wiped my mouth as Sara ran her fingers through her hair. "Is my makeup okay?" she whispered.

"Perfect," Beth said. "Mine?"

Sara peered at her as Kirk and Ross climbed up the bleachers toward us, being louder than they needed to be. "Your eyeliner is smeared," Sara said.

Beth shrieked and dove for a compact while I spread my coat out next to me so there was no room for Kirk to sit.

"Hey, Trisha." Kirk was wearing jeans and a brown leather jacket that was actually pretty sweet. He swung his leg over the bleacher in front of me and straddled it like some cowboy wannabe sitting on his metal horse. "Missed you last night at Pop's."

"Yeah, well, sorry I missed out. I heard you were a dead ringer for Britney." I popped the rest of the dog in my mouth and gave him a ketchup-y smirk. "I practiced instead. You know, that thing where you run around and kick soccer balls? Much more fun."

Graham and I had practiced after school today as well, and it had been awesome. A great workout and nothing else. None of this stupidness. I seriously doubted Graham

32

had even noticed I was a girl, and that was fine with me.

Kirk gave me an obvious once-over. "Well, you might have been sweaty yesterday, but you clean up good."

I snorted and rolled my eyes. Didn't he get that he had a much better chance with me if he appreciated my soccer talents and not my hair? Not that I cared what he thought of me, or especially how I looked.

"So, Kirk, when are you going to do a karaoke duet with me?" Sara tapped his leg with her toe. "You've got some serious dance moves."

He grinned and leaned toward her. "Anytime, babe. I think we'd be a perfect match." He slanted a calculating leer at me, like he was hoping I'd be jealous.

As if. If Sara really wanted him, and I couldn't imagine why she did, she could have him.

Ross was standing behind Kirk, looking awkward, so I took pity and tapped the seat next to Kirk with my foot. "You're blocking my view. Sit."

"Right." Ross shot a glance at Beth, who was pretending to watch the game, then sat in front of her, imitating Kirk's sideways stance so he could talk to us. "So, um, Sara, you any good at karaoke?"

Beth's mouth tightened, and Sara elbowed her. "Beth's the good singer. You should hear her sing."

"Really?" He looked at Beth, and she took her eyes off

the game long enough to look right at him.

She immediately flushed red and bent down to tie a shoe that had no laces.

I sighed and turned back to the game. Sara was nearly hanging over my lap in her attempt to flirt with Kirk, and Beth had apparently lost her ability to speak.

Whatever.

I totally should have stayed home. Watched some Major League Soccer on television or something.

I averted my gaze from them, scanning the bleachers for someone to go sit with. Anyone.

Then my heart jumped.

Graham was sitting in the next section, a few rows in front of us. It looked like there was a group of guys and girls with him, but he was sitting one row behind them, by himself. He was stretched out, his feet up on the bench in front of him between two girls, and he was leaning back, propped up with his elbows on the bench behind him.

He seemed to be ignoring everyone around him, focused intently on the game.

His jeans were faded, his sneakers were hashed, and he was wearing a Red Sox cap backward and a red sweatshirt. It was the first time I'd seen him in anything but shorts and cleats.

As I watched, he turned his head and looked right at me.

I was so surprised that I forgot to turn away and pretend I hadn't been staring.

Then he grinned and gave me a nod.

Relief rushed through me and I waved back.

"Who's that?" Beth asked, sitting up to stare at Graham. "Who are you waving at?"

Kirk twisted around to see who I'd waved at. "That guy's a sophomore. How do you know him?"

Sara shot me a weird look. "Have you been holding out on us?"

I jerked my gaze off Graham and fixed the cuff on my jeans. "His name's Graham. I practiced with him. It's nothing."

"Nothing?" Sara's eyes were wide with astonishment. "He's *hot*."

"Way hot," Beth agreed. "You really practiced with him? Alone? He's gorgeous."

Gorgeous? I took another look at Graham, who was watching the game again. Really? "He sweats a lot," I admitted. "That's cool, I guess."

"He sweats? That's all you can say?" Sara whistled. "Are you blind or something? He's a total hottie!" Then she saw Kirk frowning at us, and she immediately blushed.

"Not that he's my type, though. I mean, dark hair isn't my thing. I like blond."

No need to point out that Kirk had blond hair. Even he couldn't have been stupid enough to miss that one.

But he ignored her, taking a long look at me, then inspecting Graham, then looking back at me again, his face tight. "You dating him, Trisha?"

"No! Relax, you guys. He plays soccer. So do I. That's all it is. It *is* possible to just be friends with a guy, you know?"

Sara raised her brows, and Beth snorted her disbelief, but Kirk grinned and relaxed.

Then Sara scrambled over me and plunked herself down next to Kirk. She ran her finger along the sleeve of his leather jacket. "This leather is so soft. Where'd you get the jacket? I love it."

I had to bite my lip to keep from laughing, when Beth shot me a knowing smile. I loved Sara, but she was a total maniac around guys. And this was Kirk. So not worth her time.

But Kirk didn't buy into her thing. Instead, he looked up at me. "You going to Pop's after the game?"

"No. I'm going over to my dad's." Well, I was supposed to spend every Friday night at my dad's, but I hadn't heard from him this week, even after I'd left him the message about varsity. I had a feeling I was going to be stood up again. He'd been busy lately. Really busy. Maybe I should go to Pop's. Might be more fun than sitting home being ditched again, and having my mom make chocolate chip cookies . . . *again*.

Kirk rested his elbow over my knees. "So, how about tomorrow, then? Want to hit a movie?"

Sara made a noise of distress and I felt bad. I knew what she was feeling because that's how I felt about her and soccer: We both had what the other wanted. Maybe if I helped her with Kirk, she'd cut me some slack with practicing. So I leaned down and looked right at Kirk. "I'm not playing hard to get, Kirk. I'm just not interested in dating you."

Sara froze, Beth spun around to gape at me, and even Ross looked interested.

Kirk stared at me for a long minute, and I didn't blink. My eye itched, but I refused to give in. Then a slow grin appeared on his face. "Nice try, Trisha, but it's not going to work."

Argh!

Sara scowled, folded her arms over her chest, and turned back to the game.

"I'm serious!" I said.

He just gave me a sly look, like he was totally on to me,

then he turned back to the game and pressed his shoulder against Sara's, whispering something to her. She immediately bent her head toward him, and I felt a flash of sympathy. He wasn't ever going to like her, was he? She needed to forget about him.

Kirk casually leaned back against my knees, like they were a backrest.

I pulled my knees to the side and he almost fell over.

He raised his brows at me, and I stuck my tongue out at him. "Go lean on Ross."

He smirked, then turned away and slung his arm over Sara's shoulders, bending his head next to hers so they could whisper. She giggled, he laughed, and Beth sighed.

Oy. This was going to be a long night. I peeked at Graham, and he was watching us. I pointed at the back of Kirk's head and made a face, and Graham grinned at me. I smiled back, then realized Beth was looking at me.

"What?" I asked. "He's a friend. That's it."

"No guy who's that cute can be only a friend."

"He's not that cute! He's just a guy." When she rolled her eyes at me, I decided to check out Graham again, to see if I could see what she was freaking out about. But when I looked down at him, he was standing up, talking to Ashley Welles, one of the cutest girls in the sophomore class. She had this long, blond hair, a perfect figure, huge blue eyes . . . and so, of course, all the guys loved her. She was also one of those girls who always had perfect makeup and clothes that were right out of the pages of *Cosmo* or something.

What was Graham doing talking to her? I thought he wasn't into the girl scene.

As I watched, she turned and started walking away, *and he followed her*. Right down off the bleachers toward the concessions.

No. Way. How could he be into *her*? She was as girly as they come.

"So, that must be his girlfriend." Kirk sat down next to me with a thump, and I turned away from Graham and Ashley. He brushed his shoulder against mine. "I think I'll sit up here for a bit. You don't mind, do you?"

Sara was sitting with her back to us, her arms folded over her chest. Her shoulders were tense and I could practically feel her being mad at me. *Get over it, Sara*. It wasn't my fault he liked me, and he wasn't worth her time. I shifted away from him. "Get away from me."

"Because you don't want *him* to think we're together?"

"Ha. As if I care what he thinks." At Kirk's grin, I suddenly realized I'd given the wrong answer: By telling him I wasn't interested in Graham, he could take that to mean I was available. I felt like smacking myself in the forehead.

I'd had it with the guy/girl thing. It was going to give me a brain freeze!

Kirk scooted closer. "Give it up, Trisha. You know you like me. Stop fighting it."

"Ew." I shoved him off me and stood up, nearly tripping over Ross, who was sitting there like a dork, just listening and staring at Beth, who was pretending not to notice he was watching her. "I'm going to get popcorn."

Kirk stood up. "I'll go with you."

"No!" I started to walk away, then stopped when Kirk followed me. "Sara has something she wants to talk to you about." Sara's eyes widened in panic, and I shoved Kirk toward her. "She's been waiting all night to bring it up. Sit and listen."

Sara immediately sat up and grabbed his arm. "Um, yeah, see I had this question about . . . um . . . English. Yeah, English."

I bailed before Kirk could get away from Sara, jogging down the metal bleachers and heading toward the concessions, my sneakers squeaking with each step. With any luck, the line would be long and I wouldn't return to my seat until the game was way over.

I headed for cotton candy, because, well, what was better than cotton candy when I was in one of those moods? I took a quick glance around for Graham and Ashley, but didn't see them. So maybe they'd left.

Together. What was up with that?

I folded my arms over my chest and scowled at the back of the head of the girl in front of me. Dark hair, cropped shirt, and low-slung jeans. I felt my eyes widen as I saw the edge of a tattoo peeking out from under the waistband of her pants. There was blond hair and a halo. An angel. My parents would flip if I did that! Unless it was a soccer ball. My dad would probably support that. Assuming I ever saw him again to actually get his permission . . .

"Hey, Trisha."

I spun around. "Graham?"

He was standing right behind me, a navy letterman jacket from what must have been his old school slung over his shoulder. His hair was sort of spiky, which was new. It was a good look. I took a quick peek behind him. No Ashley. "What happened to your girlfriend?"

Urp. Had I actually asked that? Like I cared about his life on any level except soccer.

His brow furrowed and he looked behind him, like he was trying to see what I'd been looking at. "What girlfriend?"

"Ashley Welles. I saw you guys talking and . . ." I suddenly realized it sounded like I'd been spying on him. So I shrugged and turned back so I faced the front of the line. "Whatever."

He moved next to me, his shoulder brushing against

41

mine, and I caught a whiff of the scent I was beginning to recognize as his own. This time, there was no athletic undercurrent. He just smelled clean. Sort of like the woods. Pine-scented. I grinned to myself. A pine-scented practice partner. How fun.

"She's not my girlfriend. Are you kidding? A girl like her? Way too high maintenance." He grinned. "Plus, she hates sports."

"She's insane." I suddenly felt much better than I had a few minutes ago. Probably because the line was finally moving.

He took a step forward as I moved with the line. "What about the blond guy sitting with you? Boyfriend?"

"Ha. He wishes."

"Huh."

We were silent for a few minutes, and I watched as a guy came up to tattoo girl in front of me and put his arm around her waist, making some comment about how pretty her hair was. She giggled and leaned into him, fluttering her mascara-laden lashes at him. I snorted and I heard Graham stifle a laugh next to me.

I'd been right about Graham, after all. He was like me. Soccer was our world, and dating was for people who didn't have enough other interesting things to talk about. "You getting some cotton candy, or what?"

"No, actually, I'm heading out." He glanced at his watch. "Got a family birthday to attend. I just wanted to say hey."

"Hey, back." I grimaced at how wistful I sounded. So what if I hadn't had a family since my parents had split up at the start of the summer? Didn't bother me. "Well, have fun."

He nodded. "See you Monday?"

"You bet. Prepare to run a lot of laps."

"Back at ya, Trisha Perkins." Then he looked past my head and frowned. "Ashley spotted me." He sighed. "She needs to get a life." He winced visibly when she shouted his name. "I gotta bail. Later."

And then he was gone.

I chuckled as I saw Ashley run past me, trying to get Graham's attention. He didn't run away from me, did he? Nope. Because I was cool, and not girly.

When I got back to my seat, Kirk's attention didn't bug me nearly as much as it had earlier in the night.

Go figure.

4

*W*hen we were walking to the soccer field for practice on Monday afternoon, I was so busy thinking about Graham that I totally wasn't paying attention to where we were going.

"Wait a second." Sara stopped suddenly. "I thought we were practicing with varsity a week from Friday."

"We are." I took advantage of the moment to drop to one knee and crank the laces on my right cleat tighter. My shoes were getting a little too broken in. My dad was the one willing to cough up the dough for the really good cleats, so I'd texted him that I needed a new pair.

He must be out of the country or something, because

I hadn't heard from him since before the whole varsity thing had started.

"Then why are the varsity girls on our field? During our practice time?"

I glanced up at our field. "Holy cow." Sara was right. Varsity girls *were* there. *Now.* It was too soon. I wasn't ready. "They must be finishing up." *Tell me they're finishing up.*

"God, they're good," Beth muttered. "I had no idea how much better they were than us."

"They're not *that* good," Sara scoffed, but there was a slight waver to her voice. "I'm right there with them."

Coach Merrill was standing next to the varsity coach, and she pointed toward Sara and me. She and Coach Young turned to look at us, then Coach Young nodded and wrote something down on a clipboard she was carrying.

"Oh, no. Not today." My lungs got tight and a trickle of sweat dripped down my back. I wasn't ready yet.

"I think today," Sara whispered. "Kathleen and Heidi are already out there. So are a bunch of other girls from our team."

Our competition was already on the field? Not fair. I grabbed Sara's wrist. "Come on. Let's find out what's up."

"Right." We stalked forward, side by side, and I was vaguely aware of Beth running after us.

We reached Coach Merrill, but before we could ask, she introduced us to Coach Young, then said, "Coach Young wanted an early look at you guys. This isn't an official tryout, but she wanted to get a sense of where everyone was and see if there was anyone else she wanted to add to the list of potentials." She nodded at the field. "Why don't you all head down to the goal and take some practice shots?"

All I could manage was a nod, then I spun around and started jogging toward the goal. My hands were actually shaking.

"See, it's not a tryout," Beth said as we made our way out onto the field. "Today doesn't count for you guys. You're already on the list."

Sara and I exchanged glances. "Of course it counts," I said. "It always counts."

A varsity girl jogged up to me. "You're with me. Come on."

I shot a nervous look at Sara, who gave me a thumbs-up, then I followed the varsity girl. She dropped the ball between us. "I'm Lisa."

"Trisha."

"Hey. I'll play defense. Try to get past me to kick a goal, okay?"

I nodded and wiped my palms on my shorts. My

footwork was way better after two days with Graham. I could handle this.

Lisa backed up about ten feet and settled into a defensive stance.

I carved the ball with my foot and headed toward the goal. I'd just lean to the right to make her think I was going that way and then I'd go left. . . . She was there and stole the ball in less than a second.

Crud.

Lisa grinned and kicked it back to me. "Again."

I tried again.

She stole it again.

And *again*.

I wiped the back of my hand across my forehead and glanced over my shoulder. Coach Young was watching us. *Come on, Trisha.*

I lined up again, drew deep on what Graham and I'd been working on, and went for it. I made it fifteen feet, before Lisa stole it for the fourth time.

Crud.

I looked up just in time to see Sara kick a goal, her varsity defender grimacing as she picked herself up off the turf.

Great. Just great.

As Coach Merrill and Coach Young disappeared into the gym behind the last of the girls, I plunked myself down on the field and dropped my head between my knees. I was beat and completely frustrated. I'd been totally hosed by Lisa the entire practice, and I knew it. I was sunk.

Sara was bouncing all over the place, fired up after her great performance. "You weren't that bad."

I lifted my head to look at her.

She gave me a sheepish smile. "You'll do better next time, at least. You still have next Friday."

Beth sat next to me and put her arm around my shoulder. "And even if you don't do better and don't make the team, you can hang out with me on JV. That's not so bad."

I let out a deep breath. "I love hanging out with you, but I want to make varsity." I wanted it even more after practicing with the varsity team today and seeing their intensity, but it seemed so much further away now. Like, out of reach. Totally.

"What's the big deal with varsity, anyway?" Sara grabbed her shirt and rubbed the hem of it under her eyes, wiping off her smeared mascara. "I mean, either way, it's still soccer."

I frowned at her. "You're kidding, right? They're totally different."

Sara dropped her shirt back down and started running

her fingers through her hair, trying to untangle her dark curls. "Yeah, because varsity practices later and if we make varsity, we'll miss out on time at Pop's."

"Really?" Beth sat up. "You'll stop going? But what about Ross . . . and Kirk?"

"Well, I was actually thinking about that, you know?" Sara sat down in front of us and crossed her legs. "I mean, the whole point of doing soccer is to hang out, so if the three of us get split between two teams, then where's the fun?" Sara leaned forward, her gaze pinned to my face. "I was actually kind of thinking that maybe we should both drop out, since Beth's not going for varsity. What do you think?"

I was too surprised to answer. Drop out of contention for varsity so I could be social?

She grinned, a twinkle in her eye I hadn't seen before, winking at Beth. "I saw Kirk earlier today. He said he and Ross are going to Pop's tonight at six to study for the history test tomorrow. You want to go?"

Beth's face turned red. "Maybe. Trisha? You coming?"

I stared at them in disbelief. "Are you guys serious? You're worried about hanging out with Kirk and Ross instead of soccer?"

"Face it, Trisha," Beth said. "You're not going to make varsity. Those girls are so good."

I clenched my fists. "I can make it. I'll just work harder."

Sara rolled her eyes. "Trish, you have to mellow out about soccer. It's just a game. Who really cares if you make varsity?"

"I do!" I stood up, unable to take their attitude anymore. How could they not understand how important this was? "I'm going to go practice with Graham. I'll see you guys later."

"But what about Pop's tonight?"

"Can't do it." I grabbed a ball and left them in the field, too frustrated even to feel depressed about them going out without me. I mean, I didn't want to lose them as friends, but I wanted varsity too. Why couldn't they understand it?

Graham would understand . . . not that I was going to go complain to him. A guy wouldn't get all upset over a bad practice, and I wasn't about to go pathetic and girly on him. I'd seen him run away from Ashley, and there was no way I could take that kind of rejection today.

He was already on the field when I got there. He'd set up a bunch of cones all over the place in front of the goal. He smiled when he saw me. "We're practicing at this end today. Cool?"

"Yeah. Great." I dropped my ball at my feet and sighed. Did I really have what it took to make varsity, or was I kidding myself? Was I wasting my time? I mean . . . I suddenly became aware of Graham waving his hand slowly in front of my face. "What?"

He chuckled. "You were totally spacing out. What's up?"

I bit my lower lip to keep myself from blurting it out. I would *not* become a high-maintenance chick. I was going to be like a guy. Cool.

His left eyebrow cocked. "Trisha? What's wrong?"

I studied his face for a second, but he didn't turn away or start doing his hackey sack thing. He was actually waiting for me to answer him. Maybe I should. He would get it. "Can I ask you something?"

He nodded.

"Do you think I really have a chance to make varsity? I mean, we had to practice with them today and they were so much better. This one girl kicked my butt all over the field." All my frustration returned and I couldn't stop myself. "And my stupid friends think it's not a big deal if I don't make varsity, and it's driving me crazy!" He opened his mouth to answer, and I smacked my hand over his lips. "Tell me the truth. I need to know. Am I wasting my time with this varsity thing? Tell me the truth or I'll sic Ashley on you, I swear I will!" His skin was warm under my hand, and it sort of distracted me from how upset I was making myself. I cleared my throat. "Do you promise to tell me the truth?"

At his nod, I moved my hand away. He was smiling

again, almost laughing. I scowled. "What's so funny?"

"You."

I set my hand on my hips. "Why?"

"Because you're all insecure and I didn't think you ever got that way."

Oh, *great*. Now he was going to blow me off. Too wimpy. Too girly. Too annoying. "I'm not insecure," I snapped.

He simply cocked his head and looked at me. "Honestly, I think a lot of the varsity girls are better than you. . . ." He caught my arm as I started to turn away. "But that's to be expected. There aren't any freshmen on the team, are there?"

I eyed him. "No. Not unless some of us get moved up next week."

He nodded. "See? So, of course, they're going to be better than you right now. But that's not the issue. The question is whether you're one of the top two JV girls, right? Because two girls are moving up, right?"

"I guess so."

"So, that's all you need to think about. Once you make varsity, you have the rest of the season to catch up to the other varsity girls."

I pursed my lips while I considered his comment. "I guess . . ." He did have a point. I could be top two on JV, couldn't I?

He slung his arm around my shoulder and messed up

my hair. "Trisha, relax. You're a great player and we have almost two weeks to train."

I froze at the feeling of his arm around me. My shoulder was pressed up against his side, and his whole body was warm against me, and my stomach did a little flip-flop. This wasn't how it felt when Beth or Sara put an arm around me.

This was *different*.

He started walking toward the cones he'd set up, keeping his arm around my shoulders. Why was he doing that? Had he suddenly decided he liked me? That would be bad. I didn't like guys like that. Not even Graham, who Sara and Beth thought was so hot. Was he hot? Were they right? I mean, he wasn't ugly for sure . . . but hot?

He dropped his arm, and I sighed with relief. Yeah, relief. But then he put his hands on my shoulders and turned me to face him. Um, hello? Total eye contact. Was this the moment? Was he going to change our relationship and force me to run away from him?

"Trisha."

I swallowed hard. "What?"

"How bad do you want varsity?"

Varsity? That's what this was about? Good. That's what I wanted it to be about. Um, yeah.

"Trisha?"

"Varsity's all I want."

He nodded with satisfaction, like he totally heard me. Like he got me. Like I'd said what he wanted to hear. "You can make it. I know you can."

I met his determined gaze and felt all the pressure and frustration fall away from me. "Yeah, I can."

He grinned. "Then we better get to work, huh?"

"You'll help?"

"Of course."

Of course. A warm feeling settled in my belly. Graham did get me. Soccer was just as important to him as it was to me. We were a team, kinda. "I'll owe you."

"No sweat." He turned away and headed toward the cones. "Practicing with you helps my game, you know?"

Of course that was why he was helping me. Because it helped his game. Made sense. That was how it should be. See? We were good. It was still just us, doing soccer.

I lifted my chin, realizing that I wasn't feeling bummed out and frustrated about soccer anymore, thanks to Graham, and I jogged after him. "I'll kick your butt today," I announced.

He shot me a grin as he moved the cones. "You're so going down, Perkins."

"Not even!" I gave him a friendly hip check. "No mercy."

His eyes glittered at me. "No mercy," he agreed. Then

he tossed me a ball. "You have to get through all the cones and then kick a goal. Timed, as usual."

"Got it." I took my ball and headed toward my end, not even bothering to get upset that he had a longer course than I did. He was better than I was, and that was okay. It didn't bother him and it didn't bother me. It simply gave me motivation to kick his butt so he had to make his course shorter.

I dropped the ball. "Ready?"

"Set."

"Go!"

And then we were off. Adrenaline surged, my mind focused, and I charged forward, pretending Coach Young was watching me and I was going against Lisa with my varsity spot on the line. Around this cone, that one, to the end, and voilà! I slammed my ball into the upper right corner of the net a full half second before Graham's ball did. It was by far the most I'd ever beat him, and I threw my arms up in victory.

I laughed at the disgruntled look on his face. "What can I say? You inspire me. Take a lap, buddy."

He chuckled and smacked me lightly on the back of the head as he ran by. "I'm going to have to stop taking it easy on you."

I laughed as I watched him take off. He'd been

breathing hard after that run. I'd pushed him, and I'd beat him legit.

As I watched him jog around the field, I felt the tension from JV practice ease from my shoulders. Not only did Graham get me and help my soccer, but he hadn't even cared when I'd sort of wigged out on him. He was good for me.

Then my smile faded as I realized I was watching his quads flex with each step. Watching the ripple of muscles under the skin.

I immediately cleared my throat and yanked my gaze off him, totally flustered as I hustled over to take a couple of his cones away. What was wrong with me? We were soccer partners. He didn't like girls, and I didn't like guys. That's why we got along so well.

There would be no changing of the rules, even if I wanted to change them.

Which I didn't.

Because if I did, soccer practice would be over. I'd seen how he ditched Ashley. There was no way I was giving him a reason to do the same to me. I needed him, at least until the tryouts.

Which meant we were soccer buddies only.

Which meant no more noticing his quads.

End. Of. Story.

*I*t was almost dark when I walked out of the locker
room after our practice session, after a quick
shower. My hair was still wet, but why bother to dry it? I
was just going home. Who was going to see it?

I jumped down the stairs, humming to myself as I hit
the street.

"Wait up!"

I immediately stopped and turned around in time to
see Graham jogging up behind me. His backpack was over
one shoulder, and his gym bag over his other one. His hair
was sticking up straight from the shower.

"What's going on?" I shifted my weight and fiddled
with the strap on my bag.

"Where are you headed?" He fell in next to me, and I started walking again.

"Home. You?"

"My sister's picking me up at the ice-cream shop down the street. She's going to be late today, so I figured I'd grab some food there and study 'til she gets here."

"That's on my way home. I walk right past there." How often did he go there? Had I walked by him other times and not noticed? How weird would that be?

"You walk all the way home?" he asked.

I nodded. "It's only a ten-minute walk. Works for me."

"Cool."

We fell silent, and I became aware of the sound of his sneakers crunching on the leaves, and I realized I was matching my steps to his. I immediately shifted my gait to a different tempo. "So, I liked that new one-on-one drill we did today."

He caught my arm as I was about to cross the street, nodding at a car that was coming. "My brother plays college soccer and he told me about it. I asked him for some drills the other night."

His hand was warm around my arm and I couldn't stop myself from noticing.

The car passed, he dropped his hand, and headed across the street, still rambling on about soccer. I jogged after him to catch up, trying to focus on what he was talking about.

But all I could think of was the fact that Beth and Sara thought he was hot. And he'd been holding my arm.

He stopped suddenly and I almost ran into him. "So, we're here. You going to stop for some ice cream or head home?"

"Ice cream," I blurted. "I'm going to have some ice cream."

He dropped his bags on the one open bench out front. It was crowded inside, mostly with families and little kids. All the tables were taken both inside and outside, and all that was left was the bench. There was music being piped out from under the green-and-white-striped awning, but I didn't recognize it. Sounded like the kind of music my parents listened to. "I'll get the ice cream. The guy behind the counter has a brother on the soccer team, and he lets us skip the line. What do you want?"

"Chocolate with Reese's peanut butter cups would be awesome."

He grinned. "No protests of how you're on a diet and just want water?"

I snorted. "As if! You really think I'm that kind of girl? I'm totally offended."

He batted me softly on the head. "Don't worry, Trisha,

you're not like other girls. Why do you think I'm hanging with you and practicing with you? If you were like
other girls and all into that kind of girl stuff and stalking
me, I'd be gone. You're like . . . a guy with highlights."

A surge of warmth went through me. "Really? That's
so cool." A guy with highlights had to be the high-
est compliment Graham offered. Guess I didn't have
to worry anymore about whether he liked me. Question answered. I felt so much better knowing he didn't
like me.

Really. I felt better. I was pretty sure of it.

"Swear," he said. "Now, are you going to save my seat
or what?"

I put my foot up on the bench as he stood up. "I'll take
out anyone who dares take your spot."

"Thanks." He gave me his cute little salute, then ducked
inside the store.

I sighed and let my head flop against the wood, but
my cell phone buzzed before I could get my thoughts
in order. I jerked it out of my pocket, my heart skipping
when I saw who it was. I flipped it open. "Dad?"

"Hey, hon. Sorry I missed our date last weekend."

I picked at a loose paint chip on the bench. "No, that's
fine. Whatever." It wasn't like I'd expected him to be
there. "Did you get my messages?"

Graham sat down next to me and handed me a ginor-mous chocolate-dipped waffle cone the size of my head. I grinned. "Thanks," I mouthed.

He nodded and took a bite of his equally huge Oreo cookie cone.

"I didn't listen to your messages," my dad said. "I just saw you called so I called you back. Figured it was faster."

I scowled. "I left those messages days ago."

Graham watched me as he took another bite.

"Now, Trisha, don't get all defensive on me. I've been busy and this is my first free moment. Why'd you call?"

I took a deep breath and told him about the varsity thing. By the end, I was all excited again. "So, anyway, the tryouts are next Friday. You think you can come?"

"I'd love to, hon. I'll see if I have any meetings."

My throat tightened. "I really want you to come."

My dad sighed. "I know, hon, but you know it's diffi-cult for me to take time off work during the day."

"Yeah, and you can't take time off at night, either. When can you ever take time for me anymore? You move out of the house and it's like you moved out of my life. Don't you even care anymore?"

"Honey, I said I'll try to make it, okay? I just can't promise, you understand—"

Oh, I understood. "Forget it. Forget I asked. Bye, Dad." I slammed my phone shut and shoved it in my pocket.

"Problem with the 'rental units?" Graham grabbed my ice cream, which I'd forgotten I was holding, as it tipped precariously to the side. He smiled and held up my waffle cone. "Ice cream solves all problems."

I glared at it.

So he angled it and popped the end of it against my nose. "Sorry."

I snickered and wiped the ice cream off. "You are not."

"Sure I am. You better take it before I eat it."

"Pig." But I took the cone and took a bite. It was smooth and chocolaty and tasted awesome. I sighed and let the ice cream roll over my tongue. So what if my dad didn't care enough to come?

Graham leaned back next to me, his shoulder against mine as we ate our ice cream.

"So, I'm the tenth kid out of ten," he said after a while.

I looked at him to see if he was kidding. "Really? That's a ton."

"Swear." He took another bite of ice cream. "My parents never made it to any of our games. Ten kids was too many, you know? So they said if they made it to some and not others, it would be like playing favorites, so they never went to any."

I swirled my tongue around the ice cream. "So?"

"So, it didn't mean they didn't care. That's all I'm saying." He broke off a piece of his cone and popped it in his mouth.

I bit my lower lip for a minute. "You think that's all it is? That he's busy?"

He shrugged. "Once my parents forgot my birthday."

I thought of my birthday next month and wondered if my dad was going to forget. "Did you freak?"

He grinned. "I made them feel so guilty for forgetting that they gave me a huge party a week later. I was the only kid in our family ever to get a huge party."

I couldn't help but return his smile. "So, that's cool."

He nodded. "So, don't take it personally. Parents have stuff going on. Keep harassing him. He'll come around."

"You think?" I took a bite of my ice cream and thought about it. My dad *had* said he'd at least try to come.

"I know." He raised his brow. "You ever done tears on him? My sisters are brilliant at it."

I lifted my chin. "I don't cry."

He gave a nod of approval. "Good. Girls that cry drive me nuts." He shot me a look, like he was trying to see if I was still bumming. I managed another smile, but it was a little weak. He looked thoughtful for a second, like he was planning something. "Is your ice cream good?"

"Yeah, it's . . ." I hadn't even finished talking when he grabbed my wrist and pulled my cone toward him, dropping his head to take a huge bite out of my ice cream. "Hey!"

He lifted his head, licking the ice cream off his lips. "It *is* good. Want to trade?"

I eyed his cone. Oreo cookie was my second favorite kind of ice cream. "Can I try a bite first?"

"Go for it."

I bent over and took a bite, but as I was pulling away, he moved the cone suddenly and smushed it against my cheek. "Graham!" I batted his hand away, then saw the mischievous look in his eye. "You did that on purpose!"

He grinned. "Oops. Didn't mean to do that. Sorry."

"You are not!" Oh, this was a battle now! I grabbed his cone and shoved it upward, smashing it into the bottom of his chin and his throat before he realized what I was doing.

I cracked up as he jumped to his feet and danced out of my reach, ice cream dripping down his chin and over the front of his sweatshirt. "That was so overkill," he protested. "I barely got you."

"What can I say? I'm competitive." I grinned as I wiped a napkin over my cheek, clearing off the Oreo cookie ice goop. "Now that your cone has been shoved in your neck, I don't really want to trade, but thanks for the offer."

His eyes dancing, he pointed at my throat. "There's some on your shirt."

"Really?" Still laughing, I tugged my collar out from my neck and saw a little ice cream around the rim. "Good. I'll snack on it later when I'm hungry."

He chuckled and sat down next to me, crunching on his cone. "You know, as girls go, you're not too bad."

I grinned. "You're not bad for a guy."

Yeah, like, *so* not bad. He helped me deal with my dad. Practice soccer.

And he bought me ice cream.

And he made me laugh.

And he made me feel good about myself.

And he was cute. Not that I cared.

A red pickup truck suddenly pulled up in front of us and honked its horn. Graham jumped to his feet. "That's my ride. Gotta go."

I snickered at the ice cream still dripping down his shirt. "You're just afraid to take me on in an ice-cream battle. Wimp."

"Never." He paused with his hand on the door. "There's a Major League Soccer game on Thursday night. Any interest in watching it? We can learn a lot from watching their strategy. It's on cable. We can watch it at my house. My sister can pick us up after your regular practice and we'll skip our drilling session. Cool?"

If he hadn't already told me that I was a guy with highlights, I might've wondered if the invitation to go to his house was actually a pseudo date in disguise. As it was, no biggie. Glad I knew what was up so I didn't wig out. I nodded. "Should be fine. I'll check with my mom and let you know tomorrow."

"Great. See ya then." And then he hopped in the truck and was gone.

I had just leaned back in my seat and taken a big bite of ice cream when I heard a familiar voice from behind me. "Oh, my God."

I turned around to see Sara standing in the doorway of the ice-cream shop with her little brother. Her parents were still inside, cleaning up the table they'd been sitting at. Even though Sara was out with the family, she was still dressed up. Makeup, hair, and a cute outfit. I forced myself not to run my hand through my still damp, unstyled hair. "Hey, Sara. What's up?"

"Did I just hear what I think I heard?" Her blue eyes were wide—like, really wide, not just mascara-enhanced wide.

I shifted against the hard bench and tried to think of

what she was talking about. "What?"

"A date! You have a date with Graham!"

"Oh, *that*." I snorted and turned back to my ice cream. "Not at all. It's soccer. We're going to watch a game."

Sara plunked herself down next to me and yanked my cone out of my hand. "Trisha Perkins, a guy does not ask a girl to his house unless he likes her. I saw the way he looked at you." She grinned. "You, my friend, have a date, with a very hot guy." She took a bite of my cone for emphasis, grinning wider when I scowled at her.

"Sorry, Sara, but you're wrong. We're just friends."

She cocked her head. "You sound like you really believe that."

"I *know* it. He just told me I was like a guy with high-lights."

Her eyebrows went up. "Really?"

I sighed. "Uh-huh."

"Ahhhh . . ." She leaned back against the bench. "So that's it."

"So what's it? Can I have my ice cream back?"

She took another bite and then handed it back. "You like him."

"Graham? No way." I shook my head hard. Then did it again. "Not a chance."

"Give it up, Trisha. How could you not? He's totally

cute, and I saw him making you laugh. You guys have been spending how much time together?" She giggled. "Trisha Perkins has finally noticed the opposite sex. It's about time!"

"No." I said it firmly. "Our friendship is based on the fact that neither of us is into the dating thing. If I *liked* him, then he'd bail on me, so even if I was thinking of *liking* him, it would be stupid and I wouldn't do it." Would I? No. Of course not. The fact that I could still remember what he smelled like didn't mean I *liked* him.

Sara was wrong. So what if he was cute and made me laugh? I didn't like him.

I. Didn't. Like. Him.

She gave me this look that told me she wasn't buying it, but all she said was, "Want to come to Pop's Friday night? Kirk and Ross said they might be there, so I'm trying to talk Beth into going, but she's been wigging around Ross ever since I told her he likes her." She must have noticed my expression, because she added, "Please? I bet Kirk will come if you're there. Just stay 'til he comes and then you can leave, if you want."

I couldn't keep from grimacing. That didn't sound like my favorite way to spend a Friday night. "I don't think so. Why don't you and Beth just come over to my house and we can watch movies?"

"Please?" She put her head on my shoulder and sighed. "I'll owe you forever."

I snorted at the tone in her voice. "Why are you so into Kirk?"

Her face immediately lit up. "I like how he makes me feel."

"Really? But he barely even talks to you."

She lifted her head, shaking it vigorously. "Only when you're there. When it's just us, he's so nice. He makes me laugh, he compliments me and makes me feel good about myself, and he even listens when I complain about whatever's bugging me."

I stared at her, an eerily familiar feeling coming over me. "He does?" That was how it was with Graham. But that was because we were just friends, right?

She got this dreamy look on her face. "Totally."

"Wow." I sat back, my fingers tight around my cone. "I had no idea that it was like that between you guys." I also had no idea that it was the same as it was between me and Graham. Did that mean I liked him? No. It didn't. *It couldn't.* I would lose everything if I were stupid enough to like him.

"So, you'll help?" She sat up suddenly, an eager look on her face. "Will you tell Kirk that you're dating Graham?"

I jumped up in horror. "No!"

Her face got tense and her jaw jutted out. "Why not? You said you don't like Kirk. But you do, don't you?"

I shook my head. "No, no, that's not it. It's just that I don't want to say I'm dating Graham. What if it got back to him? He'd flip!"

She relaxed and gave me a speculative look. "Maybe he'd start thinking of you as more than a guy with high-lights."

"Which would be bad."

She lifted her brows. "Would it?"

"Yes." It would. Totally. It would.

So how come I suddenly couldn't stop thinking about it?

6

JV practice Thursday was the worst practice I'd
ever had. I was so nervous about my upcoming
not-a-date date with Graham to watch the soccer game
that I couldn't concentrate.

Of course, it didn't help that Sara had told Beth, and
they were both harassing me the entire practice about
how cute Graham was and how much we liked each
other and why didn't I simply make a move?

Even when I headed the ball into Sara's face, she didn't
shut up.

And then practice was over.

And then Sara and Beth forced me to blow-dry my hair

and put on makeup after practice.

And then I was in the truck with Graham and his sister.

And then we were alone in his basement, with a pizza and a couple of sodas on the coffee table.

I stood in the doorway, not quite able to make myself walk into the room. Graham stood in front of the couch, fiddling with the remote control. He was wearing jeans and boots, and he had a tee shirt on with a faded red oxford shirt, unbuttoned. His sleeves were rolled up and he looked casual, but cute.

Really, really cute.

It wasn't just Beth and Sara trying to convince me.

He was a hottie, and I knew it.

He finally found the soccer game, turned up the volume, and looked over at me, his eyebrows going up in surprise when he saw me still standing by the door. "What are you doing over there?"

"Um, just hanging out."

He tossed the remote onto the coffee table. "Well, it's kind of a long game to hang over there the whole time." He eased down onto the overstuffed denim cushions.

"Yeah, well, I'm comfortable." Not. But I didn't know where to sit. Next to him? On the couch? No, it might make him think I liked him and he'd bail on me. Or in one of the armchairs? But it might make him think I liked him and was pretending not to, and he'd bail on me.

Stand. I'd stand. Then he could just think I was whacked and that would be much better.

He opened the pizza box and I watched the steam rise from the cheese and caught a whiff of the bread and the tomato sauce. Um, yum. He pulled a piece free, and I watched the cheese stretch and stretch . . . then he slid his finger through the cheese and broke the strand and plopped the string of cheese on top of his slice.

He set it down on a plate next to him on the coffee table and looked at me. "I'm not bringing it over to you."

Oh, wow. He wanted me to sit next to him on the couch. Did that mean he liked me?

Ack! Of course not! Get a grip, Trisha!

"Is this how you treat all your guests? Forcing them to eat at the table? So rude." I managed to keep a light tone in my voice as I forced myself to walk into the room and I eased myself down onto the couch, a mere two feet from him. We were less than twenty-four inches apart!

Oh, sure, we'd been much closer so many times on the soccer field, like when we were going one-on-one and bumping into each other and shoving ourselves off each other with our hands, but I'd never noticed it.

Not like I was noticing it now.

Graham served up a couple of pieces for himself, shut

the lid, and turned up the volume. "I'm so psyched for this game," he said. "New England just traded for a new forward who's awesome. Tonight's his first start."

"Super." Obviously, Graham wasn't feeling the same buzz from sitting so close to me. Stupid Sara, for making me think of him as a guy! I was so going to kill her when I saw her tomorrow.

I managed an awkward smile and grabbed my pizza. The tip of the slice dipped downward and a hunk of cheese slipped off the end before I could catch it. It landed with a splat on Graham's foot.

We both looked down as it slowly slid off the toe of his boot and down the side, coming to a peaceful stop wedged in the off-white carpet fibers of his basement rug. Yeah, I was such the graceful girly girl. Sigh.

"Want it back?" Graham asked.

I giggled. "No, you can have it."

"Excellent. I was hoping to add a little carpet fuzz to my pizza." He reached down and picked up the piece, inspected it for a minute, then popped it into his mouth.

"That's so gross!" I burst out laughing as he proceeded to chew it, wrinkling his nose like he'd bitten into something horrid. "You aren't really going to eat that!"

He swallowed, his eyes sparkling with amusement. "Of course I ate it. It's just carpet fuzz."

I laughed. "You're disgusting." Then I sighed as I blew on my pizza before taking another bite. He *so* wasn't making the moves on me. No guy trying to impress a girl would eat carpet-fuzz pizza. It was too gross. Like I'd want him to kiss me when he had just eaten dirt . . .

Oh, *no*. I'd just put "Graham" and "kiss me" in the same sentence!

I was such an *idiot*!

How could I be stupid enough to like him? Not like him, but *like* him? I mean, he hung out with me because I wasn't into guys. It would be a total violation of our code of friendship if I started to like him!

I didn't like him. Did I? I had to know.

I subtly peeked at him. He was leaning forward, watching the television, his hair all spiky, his forearms resting on his thighs.

He glanced at me, winked, and my belly jumped in response even though he turned right back to the television.

No guy had ever made my belly flip before. Not like that.

There was no way to deny it.

I liked Graham.

He let out a whoop and slapped his hands on his thighs. "Did you see that play? We have got to practice that!" He turned to me, and his smile faded. All at once, he had a really wary look on his face, almost like he was afraid of me. It was the same look I'd seen on his face when he'd seen Ashley coming after him at the football game. I'd become another Ashley!

"Trisha?" His voice was cautious and a little strained. "Why are you looking at me like that?"

Oh, *God*. He could *tell*. How could he not? I'd been staring at him for, like, five minutes, thinking about him kissing me. *Think of a reason, Trisha!* But all I could think about was how cute he looked with his brow all furrowed. "Um . . ."

He cleared his throat and stood up. "I'm going to the bathroom. Be back in a minute." And then he vaulted over the back of the couch and sprinted up the stairs, three at a time.

It was the fastest I'd ever seen him move.

Because he was running away from me.

Argh! This was horrible!

I yanked out my cell phone and dialed Beth. She answered on the first ring. "How's the date?"

"Horrible!" I filled her in on what happened, whispering as fast as I could, watching the stairs and listening for Graham to come back. "What should I do? He's going to pull the plug on soccer, I know it!"

"Hang on." I heard her and Sara talking, but their voices were muffled, like she'd covered the phone.

I tapped my foot and flinched at each creak in the house. "Hurry up," I hissed.

Finally, Beth came back on. "You have to go into Emergency Recovery Mode."

"What's that?"

"Give him a good reason for the strange look on your face, then talk soccer. Big-time. Make him think he misread it. We'll do damage control when we meet up tomorrow. Got it?"

The door to the basement opened, and I slammed my phone shut and shoved it in my pocket. I wiped my palms on my jeans as Graham walked down the stairs, a whole lot slower than he'd gone up.

God, this was so embarrassing.

I took a deep breath, then flopped back on the couch. "Did you bring ice?"

He looked at me and paused on the stairs. "Ice? Why?"

"I burned the roof of my mouth on the cheese. It's killing me." I rolled my eyes. "Sorry I wigged you out a second ago. I was trying to assess the damage to see whether I needed to go to the emergency room, plus I was trying to figure out how to blame you for it. Not that it worked." I forced a giggle. "I'm the only idiot around here, and unless you've got ice, I think you need to call an ambulance."

"My fault? Not even." Some of the tension left his shoulders and he resumed walking toward me, hopping over the bottom step. "The soda's cold. Will that work?"

"Yeah, good idea." I grabbed a can of Diet Coke and flicked it open. "So, do you have paper and a pen? I want to take some notes tonight." I took a gulp.

He looked surprised. "Really?"

"Are you kidding?" I injected an impressive amount of excitement into my voice and set the can back on the table. "I'm so pumped for this, and I don't want to miss anything." I clenched my fists and didn't have to fake my determination. "I'm going to make varsity, Graham. No matter what."

He finally gave me a real smile. "You bet you will."

I nodded. "Now that we've both acknowledged how I'm always right, stop talking so I can concentrate on the game." I rolled my eyes. "Boys just talk and talk. Never shut up. How's a girl supposed to watch a game, huh?"

He laughed and leaned back against the couch, and I could tell that things were right between us again.

Or as right as they could be, given that I now realized I liked him, and I could never, ever, EVER admit that.

7

*S*ara and Beth were waiting for me on the school steps when I got there the next morning. Sara was checking her makeup in a compact, and Beth was munching on a bagel. They both jumped to their feet when they saw me climb out of my mom's car.

I'd been so miserable this morning that my mom had offered to drive me the short distance to school when she couldn't convince me to tell her what was wrong. As if this were the kind of thing I was going to tell her!

"You look awful," Sara exclaimed as I walked up. "Are you sick?"

"No, but thanks for making me feel better." I hadn't

slept all night, I was freaking out, and I didn't know what to do.

"Sit, sit." Sara shoved me onto the steps and opened her makeup bag. "You are in desperate need of concealer, my friend. You talk, I'll fix."

It was too much effort to keep her off me, so I gave in while Beth plopped herself next to me, munching away. "So? What happened?"

"Look up," my personal makeup artist ordered.

I inspected the sky so Sara could massage the concealer into the black pits beneath my eyes, and I filled them in on how the evening had worked out. I kept my voice low, so all the kids filing into the school wouldn't hear what I was talking about, not that they cared. It seemed like everyone else was loud and laughing and in a grand mood.

"So, that's good, then, right?" Beth asked.

"No."

"Why not? You got him back on track, right? You guys are back to the 'we don't notice the opposite sex' thing, and all?"

"She's upset because she still likes him," Sara said. "Close your eyes."

I closed them, then winced as I felt something hard on my eyelid. "Tell me you're not putting eyeliner on me."

"Oh, shush. It's about time you started wearing makeup. How else is Graham going to realize that he likes you?"

My eyes snapped open, and Sara nearly poked my eye out. "Trisha! Don't do that!"

"What did you just say about Graham liking me?"

Sara set her hands on her hips. "Oh, you look great now," she complained. "Nothing like a streak of eyeliner up into your eyebrow to make the boys fall for you."

"Sara!" I grabbed the eyeliner out of her hand and held it between my two fists. "I'm going to break this in half if you don't tell me."

"No! It's my favorite!"

She lunged for it and I jerked it out of her reach. "Talk, girlfriend."

"Fine." She pulled out a hairbrush and ran it through her hair. "All I meant was that it's obvious he likes you, but he just doesn't realize it yet. You know, because he's all anti-girl and stuff, it'll take time for him to realize it. So by making you look like a girl, maybe he'll notice that you are one." She fluffed out her hair. "Clearly, having you make googly eyes at him is not the way to approach this." She tossed the brush back in her makeup bag, then held out her hand. "Give the eyeliner back so I can finish making you look halfway decent."

"Googly eyes?" I slapped the eyeliner back into her hand. "I didn't make googly eyes! I was spacing out! Big difference!"

"Not to a guy," Sara said. "Close your eyes and don't open them until I give you permission."

I did as she instructed and tried to calm down. "Graham doesn't like me."

"Give it up, Trisha," Beth said. "Sara's the guy expert. If she says he likes you, then he does."

"If you don't shut up, I'm going to tell Ross you like him," I blurted out. I instantly felt bad, but I couldn't take one more minute of them telling me Graham liked me, when I knew he didn't. I knew it down deep in that black lump of tar in my gut.

"Fine. Be that way," Beth said.

I felt Sara rubbing on my brow, no doubt trying to erase the random streaks across my face. "So, if you refuse my help in getting him to notice you're a girl, what do you want from us?" she asked.

"It's your fault I started liking him, because you both kept talking about how hot he was, so you have to undo it. Make me not like him." That was the best plan I'd been able to come up with during my sleepless night. I hadn't been able to stop myself from liking him, so it was their problem to fix.

They didn't reply, but I could hear them whispering.

"Hello? Didn't you hear me? Fix it." I wanted to open my eyes so badly, because I had a feeling they were having a silent discussion, but I didn't want to sit there at Sara's mercy any longer than I had to. No need to drag it out by forcing another misguided streak of eyeliner. "Guys?"

"All done."

I opened my eyes as Sara stepped back. She grinned. "Nice."

Anything that was "nice" to Sara meant I needed to find a mirror as soon as possible to make sure she hadn't made me look like a clown.

Beth stood up and moved next to Sara, wrinkling her nose as she peered at me. "Well, that was stupid."

Sara and I both looked at her. "It doesn't look good?" I *knew* it!

"You look amazing," Beth said.

I raised my brows at Sara, and she shrugged. "So, why was that stupid?"

Beth shot Sara a look of pity. "Because you like Kirk. You were just starting to make progress with him, and now you go and make Trisha look even better than she does already?"

I immediately frowned. "I don't want Kirk. I don't want any guys. I just want to play soccer!"

"It doesn't matter," Beth said. "Kirk won't notice Sara unless you're out of the picture. Not with you looking like that."

Sara and I looked at each other, and she shook her head. "No, because Trisha likes Graham. You'll tell Kirk tonight at Pop's, won't you? That you like Graham?"

"No way! What if it got back to Graham?" I got cold at the thought. "He'd stop practicing with me in a heartbeat." And I needed him in my life for soccer, even if there was nothing else. Besides, as a friend, he made me feel good and I wasn't willing to give that up. To keep him as a friend, I would get over the fact I liked him. I shivered. Just thinking those words made me get all wigged out. *I liked Graham.* How stupid was I?

Sara's mouth tightened and her eyes got cool. "You won't do it for me?"

"It's not like that," I said. "I just, well, if you'd seen the look on Graham's face last night . . ."

She held up her hand to silence me. "Forget it. I understand. You'll put soccer over me, your best friend."

I jumped up. "No, I'm not! This is your fault, anyway! If you hadn't convinced me that I liked Graham and made him go all wacky on me last night, maybe I could pull off a lie to Kirk and then explain to Graham I was saying I like him just to help *you* out, but you already messed that up and he'd never believe me. So it's your fault I can't do it! Besides, it's not like I'm doing anything to try to get Kirk to like me, so don't be mad at me!"

Beth cleared her throat and moved between us. "Okay, you guys, chill out. . . ."

"I disinvite you tonight," Sara said. "Don't come. You'll just mess things up with me and Kirk."

"I don't want to go, anyway! You think it's fun for me to sit there and watch you making an idiot of yourself over him?"

Beth winced. "Trisha—"

"An idiot?" Sara gasped. "I'm an idiot? What does that mean?"

"Because you get all flirty and ditzy and weird! Did you even consider that maybe the reason Kirk likes me is because I'm normal around him? You fondle his coat and get all girly on him. Why don't you try being normal? Maybe he'd like you then!"

Her face twisted. "I *am* normal!"

"Not when you're around Kirk," I said. "I don't even like you when you're like that. And neither does Beth."

Sara sucked in her breath, her eyes wide with shock. *"What?"*

"She didn't mean that," Beth interrupted. "We both love you." Beth glared at me. "Take it back, Trisha."

"Too late," Sara hissed. "I'm out of here." Then she shoved her makeup kit in her backpack. "Don't come tonight." She turned away, ran up the steps, and let the doors slam shut behind her.

I bit my lip and suddenly felt like crying. How had that happened? I hadn't meant to say that, but it had slipped out. But she'd made me so mad! It was *her* fault I was in the mess with Graham, and all she wanted to do was make it worse by having me start rumors that I was dating Graham.

Beth picked up her backpack, her face tight. "Well, now I have to go convince her that I don't think she's an idiot around him. How could you say that? Like she's not already nervous enough around him, without you telling her that?"

"But it's true. If she acts the way she normally does, Kirk might like her. I was just trying to help. . . ."

"Well, don't try to help, then." She slung her bag over her shoulder and ran into the school, leaving me out on the steps.

I bit my lip and sat back down. I should go after them, but I didn't dare. I was so upset, I had a feeling I would just make things worse. I mean, how else could I screw up things with the only people in my life I cared about?

This is why I liked soccer. It was about the ball. About

sweat. Not about all this other stuff that was so confusing. I mean, I was just trying to get things right and now everyone was mad at me!

I sat there by myself, watching kids walk into the school, all chatting and happy, until the first bell rang and I had to go in. By the time I started up the stairs, I'd realized that due to Sara and Beth being mad at me, and Graham being afraid of me, for the first time ever, I didn't want to go to soccer practice this afternoon.

And that was the worst part of all.

That evening, at seven o'clock, I was sitting on our family room couch, wrapped up in a pink bunny comforter I'd found at the bottom of my closet. I'd left my soccer ball one on my bed. After my terrible practice, with Sara refusing to talk to me, and Beth being all uncomfortable between us, I'd wanted nothing more to do with soccer. So I'd told Graham I was feeling sick and I'd bailed.

Although he'd expressed a little concern that I wasn't permanently disabled from my bout with the pizza cheese, he hadn't seemed particularly bummed that I was ditching soccer with him, which made me feel worse.

So I'd come home, taken a package of Entenmann's chocolate chip cookies out of the kitchen cabinet, and settled on the couch with my remote at five o'clock.

And now, two hours later, I still wasn't feeling any better.

"Trisha?"

I muted *That '70s Show* and looked up at my mom. "You need me to set the table?"

"No, actually, I wanted to talk."

"Oh." I sighed and tossed the remote on my lap. "It's about Dad, right? You're worried that I'm going to develop some sort of complex because he never keeps our Friday night date?" I thought of Graham's explanation about my dad just being busy, and felt better about my dad, and worse because it made me think of Graham. "I'm fine with it."

My mom was still wearing her gray pantsuit from work at the law firm, but that didn't stop her from climbing onto the couch with me and sliding under the comforter, like we used to do before I got too busy with soccer and she got too busy doing the single-mom thing. "What'chya watching?" she asked.

"Reruns."

"Fun way to spend a Friday night."

I snorted. "Yeah, wicked fun."

She put her arm around me and pulled me next to her. "So, if it's not fun, why aren't you doing something more fun? I haven't seen much of Sara and Beth lately."

I bit my lip and said nothing. What was there to say? Instead, I snuggled against her and rested my head on her shoulder. I know, totally babyish, but I couldn't help it. I needed my mom right then. I needed someone who wasn't mad at me.

"How's the extra practice going? Is your game improving?"

My throat tightened up. "I guess."

She was quiet for a moment, drumming her fingers on the top of my head. "So, how was the game last night? With Graham?"

"I burned the roof of my mouth and accidentally dropped pizza on his carpet."

I felt her smile. "Well done, Trisha. There's nothing like making a mess to impress a guy."

"But I wasn't trying to impress him!" I wailed. "I don't want to like him! I just want it to be like it used to be, before Sara messed everything up!"

"How did Sara mess everything up?" Her voice was so calm that I couldn't hold back anymore, and the whole story came pouring out. *Everything.* "So now Sara and Beth hate me and I can't go to Pop's with them tonight, even if I wanted to, which I don't, but I can't and—" I paused to blow my nose in the fiftieth tissue I'd used since I started talking. "And I didn't even go to practice, and he didn't even care!" I started to cry again and my mom hugged me.

"Oh, sweetie, you didn't do anything wrong. . . ."

I pushed off her and blew my nose again. "But Sara's still mad. It's not my fault Kirk likes me."

She smiled and fluffed my bangs. "True, but that doesn't make it any easier for her."

"She should get over it, shouldn't she? Apologize?"

"First I have a question for you."

I sat up and wrinkled my nose at her. "I'm not going to like it, am I?"

She smiled. "You feel bad because you like Graham and he doesn't like you back, right?"

I picked a fuzz ball off my faded comforter. "Maybe."

"So, that's how Sara feels with Kirk. She likes him, but he doesn't like her back. She feels exactly like you feel with Graham, except it's worse because her best friend is the reason he won't like her." She cocked her head. "How would you feel if you found out that Graham liked Beth?"

"I'd hate her." The words slipped out before I could stop them, and I made a face.

But my mom just smiled. "See how she feels now?"

I guess I did. "But if I go in there and tell Kirk I like Graham, then . . ."

She shook her head. "No, don't do that. Just go in there

tonight and tell Kirk the truth. That you're not interested in him as a guy."

"But I already told him that. . . ."

"Make him understand you mean it."

I groaned. "How? He's totally thick."

She played with my hair. "Maybe tell him to look in Sara's direction. Couldn't hurt, right? And then you could coach Sara on how to be herself when she's around him."

I wrinkled my nose. "Why should I? She ruined my life by making me like Graham."

My mom arched an eyebrow. "I think you did that all by yourself, Trisha. And only you can fix it."

"Tell me how and I'll do it." Anything to stop me from liking him and screwing up the one good thing in my life.

"Find someone else to like."

"Mom!" I wailed. "But I don't want to like boys!"

She smiled and ruffled my hair. "Oh, kiddo, I think it's too late for that. You're in the ball game now. It's up to you to take control."

I pulled the comforter over my face. "I can't."

She pulled it back down. "At the very least, you can get your fanny over to Pop's and help Sara out. She's your friend, and you should never let a boy come between you and your friends. Girls have to stick together. It's the only way to survive boys."

"What if Graham's there? He might be there on a Friday night. What am I supposed to do then?"

She smiled and flipped the comforter off both of us, then stood up. "You'll talk soccer and let the rest go. Be yourself. Things will work out."

I frowned at her. "Things will work out? That's all the advice you have?"

"It's great advice." She laughed. "Now get up and let's go find something for you to wear that'll knock Graham's socks off if he happens to be there."

"But I don't want to knock his socks off! And that's a totally lame expression, by the way." But a little part of me liked the idea. I mean, would it be so bad if he thought I was cute? If he noticed that I cleaned up okay?

"All the more reason to do it." She grabbed my hand and tugged me to my feet. "There's a reason I always look nice when I go to work."

I kept a scowl on my face while she hustled me upstairs. "Because you'll get fired if you look like a slob?"

"Because, my little grouch, it makes me feel better on the inside if I like how I look on the outside." She gently shoved me into the bathroom. "Get in there, wash your hair, and I'll pick out some clothes. We're going to make you look like the girl you are, underneath all that sweat and dirt."

"I like dirt," I protested, even as I tugged my sweatshirt over my head.

"Of course you do. And you're welcome to roll around in the yard after we finish cleaning you up." My mom pulled the door shut.

"Promise?" I turned on the shower and shucked the rest of my clothes. "Because I will, you know."

"Oh, I know," she called out from the direction of my bedroom, where I could hear her pulling open my drawers, looking for my outfit for the night.

I grinned. My mom always looked awesome, and if she got on my case for tonight . . . well . . . I almost hoped Graham would be there.

8

At seven fifty-five, my mom was done with my makeover. We stood next to each other and studied my outfit in my bedroom mirror.

Low-rider jeans.

Uggs.

And a V-neck top that was sort of fitted. Not *tight* but not hugely baggy, either. I'd bought the shirt a year ago when I was out with Sara and Beth, and I'd never worn it. It was simply too girly. I'd bought it only because they'd *made* me.

But my mom insisted, and she'd done my hair and my makeup and even let me borrow her diamond pendant.

She smiled as she tucked a strategically dangling tendril of hair behind my ear. "I must say, I'm very impressed with myself."

"I'm going to go roll in the dirt as soon as I'm outside." My heart thudded as I inspected myself. For the first time in my life, I looked like a girl.

And you know what? I loved it. I absolutely adored how I looked.

My mom's smile widened. "Why don't I believe you?"

"I can't go into Pop's like this." I took a deep breath and tried to slow my racing heart. God, could I really do this? Walk in there looking so . . . female?

"Sure you can. You'll have a blast." She held out a little navy purse with embroidery on it. "Just bought this. You can use it."

It looked just like the purse Miley Cyrus was carrying in the latest issue of *Teen People*. I grabbed it from my mom. "You're the best!"

"I know." She hugged me, and we were both careful not to mess up my outfit. "Go have fun, okay? Just make sure that you help out Sara too."

I nodded, still looking at myself in the mirror. My new haircut looked great, with the layers falling over my face and the highlights shining in the light.

"Ah, my little girl." My mom brushed my cheek with the back of her hand. "How did you get so smart?"

I stood taller. "I'm not your little girl."

She cocked her head. "No, I suppose you're not." For a moment, she almost looked sad, then she cleared her throat. "Do you want a ride?"

"And have my mom drop me off?" I teased. "No way. I'll walk."

She nodded, her eyes bright. "I figured you would. Keep your phone on, in case I need to reach you."

"Always." That was the condition of the phone, and I wasn't about to blow it. "I'm out of here." I hesitated, then threw my arms around her. "Thanks, Mom!"

"Anytime, sweets."

Then I let go of her and ran down the stairs. To go to Pop's. Looking like a girl for the first time ever.

I was totally embarrassed, *and* I couldn't wait.

I walked into Pop's at ten after eight and nearly turned around and walked right back out when I saw how many kids were there.

The place was packed, music was roaring, and there didn't seem to be an empty seat. So many kids I knew, so many I didn't. There were tables of girls giggling and laughing, tables of guys being loud, and tables of girls and guys hanging out. I suddenly felt completely out of my comfort zone.

I hadn't been to Pop's on a Friday night in ages, and

now I remembered why.

This wasn't my scene.

At all.

Especially without Sara and Beth to back me. Where were they? I looked around but didn't see them. If they weren't here, I was so going to leave. . . .

"Trisha!"

I jerked my gaze to the right, and saw Kirk waving at me. He had one of the big booths by the window, by himself. Relief surged through me at the sight of someone I knew, even if it was Kirk.

Clutching my cute little purse to my chest, I pushed my way through the throng of kids.

"Hey." He grinned as I slid in opposite him. "I got here early to snag a table." His gaze went to my hair and I suddenly got nervous.

"Hi." I fiddled with a few strands, wishing I'd put it in a ponytail. What had I been thinking, letting my mom blow it dry?

"You look cute." He sounded surprised.

I frowned. "What's that supposed to mean?" Was he making fun of me?

He shook his head once, his gaze traveling over my face, my outfit, and even my purse. "I just . . . I mean . . . you don't look like you normally do."

I folded my arms across my chest. "So?"

"So, I like it."

I studied his face for a long moment, but his gaze was steady. I realized that he meant it. I really did look okay. My body relaxed and I leaned back. "Well, then, I guess, thanks."

He nodded. "I'm going to get a drink. Hold the table?"

"Sure." I cleared my throat. "So, um, are Sara and Beth coming, or what?"

"Yeah." He slid out of the booth to his feet, his gaze flicking to my hair again. He shook his head slightly, like he couldn't quite believe what he was seeing. "So, you want something to drink?"

I grinned at his reaction. "Diet Coke. Get a pitcher. That's what Sara and Beth drink too." Sara . . . I needed to deal with that. I mean, I should tell him, now, that Sara likes him. "Um, Kirk, about Sara . . ."

Suddenly I lost my train of thought when I noticed Graham walking toward us, carrying a couple of drinks. He glanced at me, and his eyes passed over me, then his gaze snapped back to my face, his eyebrows nearly shooting off his forehead.

"What about Sara?" Kirk prompted.

I waved him off. "I'll tell you later. I'm really thirsty. Go get me something to drink. Please," I added.

He shrugged and headed to the counter, giving Graham

a second look as he walked by him, like he was trying to place him.

Be cool, Trisha. It's all about the sports.

Graham headed straight toward my table, his gaze pinned to my face.

I held my breath and sat straighter as he approached. I could totally handle this. Really.

9

*G*raham paused at my table, his eyes scanning my outfit like crazy. "Hey," he said. He was wearing baggy jeans with a hole in the right knee, a black tee shirt, and a black leather jacket. Um, hello? Hottie alert. Since when did he own a leather jacket?

"Hey, yourself." I shifted in my seat and clenched my hands under the table, where he couldn't see them.

"Feeling better?"

"Yeah, I'm feeling better. I crashed when I got home for a few hours. But I'm really wigging that I missed practice. I'm going to head over to the school in the morning to drill. You in?"

His gaze flicked to my diamond pendant. "Um, I don't know. . . ."

I shrugged. "Whatever. Just thought I'd throw it out there. I was going to practice some of those moves we were talking about last night, during the game." *Talk soccer. Talk soccer.*

A fresh light came into his eyes and he slid opposite me. "Which ones?"

Caught a whiff. He smelled good. I refused to notice. "That offensive move where the guy faked out the defender when he . . ."

"Right." He nodded. "That was slick. And the one right at the end of the game where he passed the ball . . ."

"Well, duh, of course that one." We'd talked about that play for at least ten minutes. "So, that's cool if you're not into it, but I was thinking I'd ask Sara and Beth to help me, if you can't make it."

He drummed his fingers on the table. "What time?"

"Ten?" I smirked at him. "I suppose that's too early for an old guy like you."

His eyebrows went up. "Old? I'm a year older than you."

"I know. You got any gray hair yet?" I reached over and pretended to pluck one from his head. "Got one."

He grabbed my wrist and tugged my hand away from

his head. "Cut it out, you crazy chick." But he was laughing, looking at me the way he always did. He tightened his grip around my wrist as I tried to get it free. "Fine. I'll practice tomorrow. I can't leave you on your own. You're too dangerous to yourself." I stuck my tongue out at him and he leaned forward to peer at it. "Looks like the burns are healing well. No need for emergency tongue surgery."

"No thanks to you."

"Me?"

"You bought the pizza, so it's your fault." I giggled as he tried to put on an offended face. "Oh, give it up, Graham. You're so not innocent. . . ."

Someone cleared their throat and we both looked up. Kirk was standing there frowning at our hands.

We followed his gaze, realizing at the same time that Graham still had his hand wrapped around my wrist.

We jerked our hands back, and Graham slid out of the booth, his face suddenly wary again. Oh, *great*. Back to that already? He'd been the one holding on to me!

"Okay, so, see you later, Trisha," Graham said. He nodded at Kirk. "Later." He grabbed his drinks and bolted.

I tried to watch where he went, but Kirk moved into my line of vision as he sat down. So I craned my neck to see around him, relocating Graham just in time to see him sit down at a table full of guys at the back.

No, wait. It wasn't just guys. There were *girls*. I sat up straighter, my heart starting to pound. Did that blond hair belong to Ashley? Was he at Pop's with *Ashley*? I clenched my fists as I saw her turn to the side so I could see her profile.

Yep. It was Ashley. And she had her hand on Graham's arm. And he wasn't bolting! What was up with that? Since when did he like girly girls? Did he actually like them and he was just pretending to hate them as a reason not to like me? Was it *me*, then, that he didn't want that kind of relationship with?

I felt sick. Totally sick.

"Trisha?"

I dragged my gaze off the train wreck at the back of the room and looked at Kirk. "What?"

"You okay? You look kinda strange."

I took a deep breath, which was totally shaky. "I'm fine."

He slid the pitcher and a glass of ice toward me. "That's the guy from the football game, right?"

"Uh-huh." I tipped the glass and managed to pour the soda without spilling it all over the table. Was Graham still there with Ashley? Was his arm around her? Was he looking at me? I wanted to know. Had to know. Refused to turn around.

"So, um, he keeps looking over here," Kirk said.

"Really?" I grinned, but I didn't look at Graham. No way was he going to catch me looking at him.

Kirk leaned back in his seat. "So, you said you guys weren't dating, but that's not true, is it?"

I snorted. "Oh, it's true." I took a long drink of soda and eyed the window we were sitting next to, trying to see if I could see Graham in the reflection. Was that his table? Yes, yes, it was! Right on!

Then my gut sank. Was his arm really around the back of Ashley's chair? It couldn't be! Must be a distortion from the reflection. I looked at Kirk. "Is his arm around the back of that girl's chair?"

Kirk looked at me for a long moment, then he turned in Graham's direction. "Yeah, it is."

I pressed my lips together and tightened my grip on my cup.

"So, that's how it is." He sounded resigned.

I stared at the little bubbles on the surface of my soda, watching each one pop. *You will not look at Graham.* "How what is?"

"You have a crush on him."

I jerked my gaze to Kirk's. "What? No way! Hah. That's totally stupid!"

He lifted his brows.

I lifted mine right back.

For a minute, we had an unspoken eyebrow-lifting contest, then I grinned. "You win. I'm getting a headache."

He smiled and let his brows drop down. "So, you really meant it on the field that day when you said you weren't into me?"

I shrugged.

"Huh." He shifted in his seat. "So, maybe I should hit the road, then. Before the others get here."

He started to slide out of the seat and I grabbed his wrist. "Wait!"

"Trisha—"

"What do you think of Sara?"

He looked at me blankly. "Sara? She's nice, I guess."

"But is she cute?"

His forehead wrinkled slightly. "Well, yeah. Of course."

Oh, she was so going to kill me for this, I knew. "She really likes you."

He stared at me, his eyes wide. "What?"

"See, that's one reason why I never thought of you as a guy. I couldn't! She's liked you forever and I'd never do that to her."

He leaned back in his seat with a thump, staring at me. "You're kidding. Sara? But she's such a flirt. I didn't think she meant anything by it. . . ."

"She's that way only with you." I rolled my eyes. "Seriously, Kirk, give her a chance. She's actually really normal.

She just wigs around you because she likes you."

"Wow." He rubbed his chin, a thoughtful look on his face. "Wow."

I leaned forward. "So? Do you like her, then?" On second thought, she wasn't going to kill me. She was going to love me forever for this one.

He grimaced ever so slightly. "She's not really my type, you know?"

Oh, *no*. "But she's cute and friendly. . . ."

"Does she ever sweat?" He rolled his eyes. "That's why I like you, Trisha. You're cool. You're into sports. I dig that."

"But *you're* not into sports. All you do after school is hang out at my practice. That's why I can't like you. I can't be with a guy who's less of an athlete than I am."

He shot me a cocky grin, his eyes suddenly sparkling. "Before you judge me, you might ask me if I play any sports."

I frowned. "Do you play any sports?"

"Ice hockey."

Surprise made my mouth drop open. "You do? When?"

He pulled the straw out of his drink and began to twist it around his finger. "Well, as you probably know, our school doesn't have ice hockey, so I play in a private league year-round. We have ice time at five A.M. every day, and play games on Sunday afternoons."

"Really?" I leaned forward, interested in what he had

to say for the first time ever. "Are you good?"

He shrugged. "I'm okay."

"Which means either that you're terrible or that you're great and you're too humble to admit it." I cocked my head. "Knowing you, I tend to doubt the humble thing, so you must not be very good. . . ."

He grinned. "Actually, I went to Canada last winter to play in some tournaments over the Christmas holiday."

"Really?" I drummed my fingers on the table, feeling like I was looking at him for the first time ever. His eyes were sort of a dark green and his eyelashes were long. Interesting. "That's so cool. I had no idea. I thought you were just this guy with nothing going on in his life other than torturing me."

His smile got a little strained. "I torture you?"

"Well, yeah, usually. Right now, you're almost tolerable, though." I sat up, wrapping my hands around my drink. "So, tell me about Canada. Did you play Canadian teams or was it tournaments, or what?"

"You really want to know?" he asked, sounding surprised. "Most girls don't really want to hear about hockey."

"I do." I leaned my elbows on the table and propped my chin up in my hands. "I think it sounds awesome. I'd love to be good enough to play in other countries. That's my goal, you know. To be able to play college soccer, then go international. But you're already doing it." I sighed, gazing at him. "That's so cool. How long have you been skating?"

A genuine smile softened his face and he shoved his drink out of the way and leaned forward, clasping his hands on the table. "Well, I started when I was six. . . ."

Twenty minutes later, we were deep in conversation about sports when Kirk suddenly stopped talking and looked at me.

Uh-oh. Did I have mascara on my eyelid or something? "What?"

"You want to go on a date sometime? A real date?"

Oh, wow. I sat back and looked at him. I mean, I was having a blast talking to him and he was cute and every-thing, but, well . . . he wasn't Graham.

He leaned forward. "I mean, we're having fun, right? Getting along?"

"Yeah." And we were. I should like him. I should. There was nothing wrong with him.

"So, let's try it."

"Well . . ." No. I couldn't do it. I just didn't want to. I was simply too into Graham, and going on a date with Kirk wouldn't fix it. Besides, I couldn't do that to Sara even if I *did* like him.

"Trisha?"

I cringed and looked up. Sara was standing right next

to the table, a look of disbelieving horror on her face. "Sara! Kirk and I were just talking about you. . . ."

"Yeah, I heard. Was that before or after you told him how cool he was for being a hockey player? Before or after he asked you out on a *date*?" Her voice was cold and I saw Kirk's eyes widen.

Beth stood behind her, looking way uncomfortable. "Um, so, what's up, guys?" Her gaze darted around the room. "Is . . . Ross here?"

"He's coming," Kirk said, still staring at Sara, who looked like she was about to explode. There was a definite thoughtful gleam to his eye—the kind a guy gets when he's just been told that a girl is in love with him. Like, "Oh, here is one of my adoring fans."

"Come to the bathroom with me. We need to talk," I said, trying to catch her eye.

"No. Way." Her eyes flashed with anger. I'd never seen her so mad. "You just lost me as a friend, Trisha Perkins. I will kick your butt on the soccer field next week, and you are so going down." She spun around. "Come on, Beth."

Beth shot me an apologetic look. "Call me later," she mouthed. "We'll talk." And then she hurried after Sara.

Crud. I dove out of the booth and grabbed Sara's arm. "Wait!"

She whirled to face me. "How could you do that? How could you go for him? You know I like him!"

"I didn't go for him!" I lowered my voice, knowing Kirk was only a few feet away, but the place was so loud that I prayed he wouldn't be able to hear me. "I told him you liked him!"

"What?" She screeched. Kirk could totally hear *that*. "How could you do that? I'll never be able to look at him again!"

"But, I thought that's what you wanted me to do. . . ."

"Forget it, Trisha. You are so history." She pointed at me. "Don't you dare follow me or I swear I will climb up on that table and scream to everyone that you're in love with Graham Fordham."

I dropped her arm and sucked in my breath. "You wouldn't!"

"Oh. I *would*. And for your information, Graham is outside right now, kissing Ashley Welles."

I recoiled in horror, my hand going to my mouth. "*What?*"

She leaned into my space and glared at me. "Stay out of my life, Trisha Perkins, and prepare to kiss your spot on varsity good-bye. You take what I want, and I'll take what you want." And then she was gone, Beth running after her.

I didn't dare follow her. Not with that threat.

But she had to be lying. Graham would never kiss Ashley. Never! But when I looked back at Graham's table, he wasn't there. And neither was Ashley.

Oh, God. Had Sara been telling the truth?

My stomach churned and I sank back onto the seat across from Kirk.

He eyed me, looking way too amused by the whole situation. Why wouldn't he? Two girls in a screaming fight over him? Of course he'd think it was hilarious. I glared at him, and all he did was smile. "So, I'm thinking that you and me on a date . . . not a great idea, huh, Trisha?"

"Gee, you think?"

His smile widened. "So, about Sara . . ."

"What?" I snapped. I had to get home. This night was a disaster.

"I had no idea she could yell like that. It was a good threat, too. Think she can pull it off?"

I stared at him. "You like her now because she yelled at me?"

He shrugged, still looking *way* too happy. "I didn't realize she had it in her. Is she really going to kick your butt on the soccer field?"

How could he sound so cheerful? I stuck my tongue out at him and left.

I'd had *enough*.

10

I almost stayed home from practice with Graham the next morning, but Sara's threat kept hanging over me like a bad grade. If she really decided to bust her butt on the soccer field, I was in such trouble, especially since I already had one bad tryout.

Forget Sara. She was going down.

I was already drenched in sweat by the time Graham arrived a little after ten. I was burning my way through some drills and I had my back toward that side of the field, but I suddenly knew he was there. It was like my bones got all tingly and my pulse jacked up.

He said nothing, and I didn't turn around. All I could think about was him with Ashley. Had he left with her?

Why had he let her put her hand on his arm? Was all his anti-girl sentiment actually a lie? Was it just me he didn't like? Had he really kissed her?

Scowling, I slammed the ball at the net. It careened over the top of it and sailed into the next field. Crud.

"Nice shot."

Was he sarcastic with Ashley too, or was I the only lucky one? "Thanks," I snapped, jogging after my ball to retrieve it. I picked it up and turned around, almost stopping at the sight of him.

He was wearing navy sweats and a fleece against the brisk morning air, and he was wearing a baseball cap on backward. So casual, so cute. So unfair.

"So, want to do some passing drills this morning, then?" he asked, not even giving me the slightest inspection.

"Yeah." I walked up and dropped the ball at his feet. "Sounds good."

He cocked his head. "Good morning to you, Ms. Cranky."

"Good morning to you." I ignored the remark about my mood, because, well, he was right. I was being a grouch, and it wasn't like I was going to tell him the reason. What was I supposed to say? Ask him whether he was dating Ashley?

"Are you dating Ashley?" Oh, *crud*! How had that slipped out?

113

Graham looked startled. "Ashley? You're kidding, right?"

I grabbed the ball with my toe and headed away from him to start the passing drill. "You were there with her. She was all over you and you didn't seem to mind." I kicked him the ball and started running down the field.

"All over me?" He slammed the ball, and I had to sprint to catch it before it sailed past me. "She and her friend had a table and they let us join them when there were no other open ones. Not a big deal."

I cut in front of him and he passed me the ball as he split in the other direction. "Well, she had her hand on your arm. What's up with that?" I kicked the ball ahead of him and felt a mild sense of satisfaction when he grunted and dug in to try to catch up to it.

"I don't even remember. What's it matter to you?" He was breathing heavily as he dribbled the ball a few feet, waiting for me to move into position.

"It doesn't matter, except Kirk was convinced you and I were dating, even when I denied it." I ran across the field and nodded for the pass. "So when he saw you and Ashley getting it on, he thought I was all pathetic because you were hanging with her in front of me." Not quite the truth, but close enough if he wanted to hear what I was really saying.

Graham smashed the ball at me and I had to head it to

keep it from sailing past me out of bounds.

"Sorry," he muttered, blocking the ball and trying a much more controlled pass right to me. "Ashley asked if you and I were a couple."

My cleat caught in the turf and I almost went down. "*What?*" I regained my balance and dribbled a couple of yards while Graham sprinted toward the goal. "You and I? As if!" I lifted the ball up, toward Graham's face. "Did you kiss her?"

He scowled and headed the ball into the upper right corner of the net. Then he spun toward me, his hands on his hips. "Did you just ask me if I *kissed* her?"

I eased to a stop in front of him. "Did you?"

His cheeks turned red and my gut tightened in dismay. Was that a guilty look? "Graham! Why didn't you tell me you were dating her? I thought we were all bonding over our 'we aren't into the dating scene' thing, and then I find out that you're dating her?"

"I didn't lie to you," he protested. "I said I wasn't dating her, and I'm not. I'm not dating anyone."

"But did you kiss her?"

"Why does it matter to you?"

"Because I thought you were my friend, and friends don't lie to each other. I trusted you because I thought you were like me. Not into dating. We made fun of people who got stupid around the opposite sex. Was all that a lie too?"

"No! I'm not dating her!"

I folded my arms over my chest, well aware that he was avoiding the bigger question. "Did you kiss her?"

He turned away to go retrieve the soccer ball that was still sitting in the back of the goal. "She kissed me when we left," he muttered. "It was nothing. Friends. I didn't kiss her back."

"Friends?" Oh, God! My stomach was killing me and I felt this weird buzzing in my ears. "You don't kiss someone that you're only friends with! What kind of stupid comment is that?"

He grabbed the ball and spun toward me, a scowl on his face. "It's not the same kind of kiss, trust me."

"Was it on the lips?"

His cheeks got even redder. "That's not the point."

"It *is* the point." I marched up to him and poked him in the chest. "If you kiss a girl on the lips, it's not a friends kiss. It's a dating kiss."

"It doesn't have to be."

"Of course it does!"

His eyes narrowed, and I realized I'd gone too far, riding him over Ashley. *Come on, Trisha! Get it together!*

Then he suddenly dropped the ball, set his hand on my shoulders, and pulled me toward him. Before I even knew what he was doing, he bent his head and kissed me.

116

On the lips.

Oh. My. God.

His lips were soft and warm and he tasted like mint toothpaste, and my belly jumped like a mile. His fingers tightened on my shoulders and I instinctively grabbed his wrists as he kissed me *again*, so gently, so soft, so *perfect*.

He tilted his head, his breath hot against my lips. A chill shot down my spine and I kissed him back. *This* was how a kiss was supposed to be. It was amazing and perfect and awesome and I would never, ever, ever forget this moment.

Then suddenly he froze and his lips stopped moving. So I froze too.

He broke the kiss and looked down at me, his hands still gripping my shoulders, his eyes all dark and intense.

I stared at him, my lips tingling and my body all freaking out.

He cleared his throat. "See?"

I wet my lips, trying to get my brain working again. "See what?" *That you like me? That that was the best kiss in the history of the world?*

He took a breath. Then another one. "A guy and a girl can kiss on the lips and it can be a friends kiss."

I blinked as his words sank in. "A friends kiss?"

"Yeah." He dropped his hands from my shoulders and

sort of shook out his shoulders. "See? We kissed. It meant nothing, because we're just friends." He sent me a sideways glance. "Right?"

Depression settled like a black cloud in my mind as I realized what he meant. The kiss had meant nothing. He'd kissed me to prove a point. To win an argument.

But it had been so perfect! How could it have meant *nothing*? It had been my first kiss! First kisses were supposed to be perfect! They weren't supposed to mean *nothing*!

"So?" His voice sounded a little ragged. "You take back your comment about Ashley now?"

I gaped at him, struggling to get my mind together. Should I kick him in the shin? Cry? Leave? "You have no right to kiss me!"

He frowned. "It wasn't that kind of kiss. It was just a kiss."

Just a kiss. This was horrible! He was so not into me that he'd kissed me, I mean *really* kissed me, and he obviously hadn't felt even the faintest spark of *anything*.

He wasn't into me.

He wasn't into me.

My throat tightened up and my eyes suddenly got all watery. Ack! I wasn't going to let him make me cry! I jerked free of him and spun away, blinking as hard as I could. "So, yeah, so Sara is going to try to beat me out at varsity, so I have to, um, practice, really hard this week, because, you know, I don't want to, like, not make it, you know?" The ball was blurry, but I grabbed it and started heading back up the field. "So, um, I think, like, yeah, maybe, so, run that drill another time?"

When he didn't answer, I turned around. He was standing where I'd left him, the strangest look on his face as he stared after me.

"What?" I snapped.

"The friends thing," he said. "You buy it now?"

"Oh, yeah, sure. That kiss makes it clear. No magic. Whatever. Can we practice now?"

For a long moment, I thought he wasn't going to answer, then he nodded and seemed to kick into gear again. "Sure. Let's do it." He jogged past me, flicked my ponytail, and kept running.

Great. We were back to the ponytail-flicking relationship. It was the perfect foundation for another week of practice.

But as I squared up with the ball, I began to seriously doubt whether I could take another week of practice with him, even for the sake of varsity.

Because I just couldn't get that kiss out of my mind.

11

*M*onday was the worst day of my life. Sara ignored me all day, and Beth tried to be neutral. And practice was the worst. Sara knocked me to the ground three times and played the best I'd ever seen her play. Even with how much I'd improved during the time I'd been practicing with Graham, she was still better than I was.

I was peeling my face out of the dirt for the third time when Beth squatted next to me. "You okay?"

"Great." I spit some grass out of my mouth and sat up.

"You might want to apologize. That would help."

"Apologize? I was trying to help her!"

Beth picked something out of my hair and tossed it on the field. "Well, she doesn't see it that way."

"Gee, you think?"

She looked past me. "Especially when Kirk showed up to practice again to watch you."

"What?" I twisted around to peer behind me. Sure enough, Kirk was lounging on the sidelines, wearing his Nike shades and his usual jeans. Ross was standing next to him, kicking his toes in the dirt and shooting periodic glances at Beth. Those two *really* needed to get together. "Great. Like that's all I need is to have Kirk here to bug me . . ." But as I studied him, I realized he wasn't looking at me. He was studying the field where the action was.

I turned to look in the direction he was gazing, and my heart skipped. He was looking at Sara! *No way*. But he definitely was.

Grinning, I stood up and dusted myself off, watching Sara sprint around like someone had given her a bad haircut and ruined her life. She had no idea Kirk was watching her. She was simply being a pain in the butt to destroy me.

"What are you looking at?" Beth asked.

"Kirk. He's here to see Sara, not me."

"Nuh-uh . . ." Then she faded to quiet as she saw what I was seeing. "Wow. She has no idea. I'll go tell her."

I grabbed her arm before she could move. "No. Kirk only liked her when she forgot about impressing him and stopped being a stupid, flirty girl. If you point it out, she'll go all weird on him again."

Coach Merrill blew her whistle, signaling the end of practice, and I saw Sara shoot an evil glance at us before marching over to help Coach round up the soccer balls. My jaw tightened when I saw her chatting up the coach. She never talked with Coach. Ever. She was doing it just to get on the team, just to displace me from varsity. "I never tried to take Kirk from her, but she's trying to steal my dream."

Beth shot me a look, but said nothing. What could she say? She knew I was right.

As we watched, Kirk sidled up toward Sara and started helping her pick up the balls. She jerked her gaze toward him, then grinned, then said something and he laughed, his gaze latched on to her face like she was all he needed to survive. I pressed my lips together at the sight of their little bonding. I wanted Graham to look at me like that, just one time, even. I wanted him to walk up and be all cool and casual, even after finding out that I liked him.

"Look at that. Kirk ditched Ross. You think I should go keep Ross company?" Beth was watching Ross with the most pathetically wistful look on her face I'd ever seen.

"Yeah, you should. Go talk to him."

"Okay." She nodded once, ran her fingers through her hair, and then trotted over to him. He gave her a shy but totally adoring grin when he saw her approaching him.

And I stood there, alone, watching my friends make these guys smile, and I knew what I had to do.

I marched over to "our" field and there he was. Kicking goals while he waited for me. *Enough!* He was adorable and funny and talented and I simply couldn't take it anymore.

Graham glanced over at me and grinned. "Hey."

I took a deep breath and walked toward him.

His smile faded. "What's wrong? You look ticked off."

"I can't practice with you anymore."

He frowned. "Why not? This is the big week. Crunch time."

"I know, but I'm going to do it on my own."

His frowned deepened. "Why?"

"Because I am." I started to turn to leave, then hesitated at the look of confusion on his face. Over the last couple of weeks, he'd become my friend, and I owed him an explanation of some sort. It wasn't his fault he was an idiot. So I caved. "Here's the thing, Graham. That kiss was way out of line."

He grimaced. "But I said it didn't mean anything."

"Exactly."

A little furrow formed on his brow. "So?"

I shook my head, not quite willing to actually lay it out there. I mean, it was one thing to hint at it, it was another to announce I liked him, and I wasn't interested in being treated like a leper from the guy I considered my friend. "So you changed the rules when you kissed me, and I can't go back."

He cocked his head. "Why not?"

I poked him in the chest. "Because you're wrong. A girl and a guy can't kiss on the lips and have it mean nothing, okay? Not a kiss like that."

He stared at me, as a look of shock started to fill his face. "Are you saying that you liked my kiss?"

"That's not the point!"

"But did you?"

"Forget it!" I threw my hands up in the air and started stalking back toward the gym. I could *not* have this conversation.

Graham was beside me in, like, one second. "Can you stop walking for one minute? We need to talk."

"What's there to say?"

"Do you . . . like me? Like, *like*?" he asked.

I heard the hesitation in his voice and I bit my lower lip. This was it. The end of our friendship. I could already feel him drawing away. I took a deep breath, steeled my resolve, and then turned to face him.

His eyes were wary, and he wasn't touching me.

He looked so cute, so awesome, and all I wanted to do was say yes. To tell him the truth.

He took a step backward, away from me. "Do you?"

I lifted my hand and he flinched and backed up another step, in case I was planning to touch him.

My throat tightened up, but I had my answer. There was only one response I could give him if I had any pride. So I set my hands on my hips and met his gaze. "Graham, I think you're a great soccer player, and I enjoy hanging out with you, and yeah, I think you're a decent kisser."

His skin took on this greenish tinge and he shifted his weight, shoving his hands deep inside his pockets.

"But, quite frankly, you're not my type."

Relief cruised over his face, making me want to bury my head in a pile of leaves and cry. "That's *great*." He chucked me on the shoulder. "You had me worried for a minute. Don't mess with me like that. I can't take it."

I started walking toward the gym again, noticing that Sara and Beth and their boys were hanging out in a little foursome by the field. I could hear their laughter, and it made me feel even more alone. So I shot Graham a haughty look. "You're delusional if you think I could ever be interested in you." I laughed, even as my heart was breaking into tiny little pieces. The varsity girls were walking in the opposite direction of me, toward the field. I wanted to be with them. If I were with them, Graham wouldn't matter anymore.

His shoulders relaxed at my words, and he fell in next to me as I walked. Then after a minute or two, he cocked his head. "What's so wrong with me?"

I rolled my eyes while I tried to come up with a reason that he'd believe. "Because . . . you're like a girl."

His eyebrows shot up. "*What?*"

I coughed to stifle a laugh. "You're like one of my girlfriends, except you like sports as much as I do. I can talk about anything with you, and we have fun and stuff." I nodded. "Yep, you're like a girlfriend with hairy legs."

"A girlfriend with hairy legs?" he repeated, his voice slightly elevated.

"Yeah. And you smell worse than girls after soccer, but other than that, it's pretty much the same." I had to turn away from the look of horror on his face so he didn't see me crack up. Pride salvaged, I guess. I yanked open the door to the gym and he grabbed it as I stepped inside.

He was looking at me, like he couldn't quite figure me out. "You're some kind of piece of work, Trisha."

I managed a cheeky grin that I didn't believe. "With compliments like that, is it any wonder you're like a girlfriend? That's not the kind of thing a guy would say to a girl."

He frowned, but didn't reply.

Inside, all I wanted to do was shrivel up and die. It was over between us. We'd kissed, it had been awesome, and he *still* wanted to run away from me. The only thing that salvaged our relationship was the fact I'd called him a girlfriend with hairy legs.

How truly pathetic. I stopped outside the girls' locker room, where I could hear my teammates laughing and giggling. "I gotta go."

He grabbed my arm before I could open the door. "Why? Why are you ditching me this week? Just because of a kiss? I don't get it. I didn't think you were the type to get all worked up about things like that."

I looked at him, with his brown hair all messed up and his intense green eyes, and for the first time wondered what I was doing liking him. I mean, seriously, should I really waste my time liking a guy who would freak out at the thought of me liking him? A guy who hadn't noticed I was a girl even after I was dressed like a total babe on Friday night?

It was time to stop liking him. I deserved more than to have to spend time around him, watching every word I said in case I scared him off, being miserable because I couldn't stop liking him and he didn't like me. "Oh, I'm a girl, Graham. You just haven't noticed." Then I shoved open the door to the locker room and let it slam shut in his face.

12

*T*he next two days were even worse. I avoided Sara and Beth, and ducked into the bathroom once when I saw Graham walking toward me when I was on my way to English class. I arrived at the last second to classes and took off at the first minute the class was over, so Sara and Beth wouldn't have to make up a reason not to talk to me.

I went to practice. I busted my butt. And I tried not to notice Kirk and Ross there, cheering on Sara and Beth.

I didn't go to the field where Graham and I used to practice. I wanted to sneak over to "our" field to see if he was waiting for me. I wanted to, so badly.

But I didn't.

I couldn't. Hanging out with him right now . . . I couldn't take it.

The thought of spending time with him and not having him even acknowledge I was a girl . . . it was just too awful.

So I talked my mom into buying me a bunch of cones of my own, and I took a couple of balls and cones and practiced at the middle school on Tuesday and Wednesday. It sucked, I was so lonely, but I wasn't about to give up on varsity, and I couldn't bear the thought of all my friends and Graham seeing me by myself, like some pathetic loser.

So I was a pathetic loser in private. Much better.

I was so bummed out that it didn't even help when my dad stopped by the house to drop off new cleats for me. I knew my mom must have called him and told him how miserable I was, so he'd brought the shoes.

All it made me do was think of Graham—how he'd said that my dad probably really did care but was just too busy.

I needed my dad, and he'd delivered, just like Graham had said.

Wednesday night, I was sitting on my bed, picking grass out of my new cleats, and I thought of calling Graham to tell him that he'd been right about my dad. Graham would want to know. He'd be happy for me.

I picked up my phone and pulled up Graham's number.

Stared at it.

Then hung up.

Polished my cleats.

Eyed my phone.

Opened it again.

Pulled up Graham's number.

Then I hit SEND.

Then I disconnected and threw my phone on my pillow. I needed to stop obsessing!

It rang five seconds later, and I dove for it, my heart jumping when I saw it was Graham. I flipped it open. "Hello?" My voice sounded breathless, and I cringed.

"Did you just call?"

I flopped back on the bed at the sound of his voice. Deep, soft, perfect. "Yeah. I was just going to tell you that my dad surprised me with new cleats for tryouts on Friday."

"That's awesome." I could hear the smile in his voice, and suddenly I felt totally upset again. I *so* wasn't over him. "See? Nothing to worry about, Trisha."

"Yeah." I twirled my hair around my finger. "So, that's it. I'll, um, talk to you later."

"Wait!"

I put the phone back to my ear. "What?"

"Listen, Trisha, I screwed up with the kiss thing, and I'm sorry."

I said nothing. What was there to say?

He groaned and I heard something crash, like he'd kicked something over. "Come on, Trisha. Can you cut me a little slack? I want to be friends. Can't we be friends?"

Friends. What an ugly word. "I don't think so. Not right now."

"Give it tomorrow. We'll practice and see how it goes. You do want to make varsity, don't you?"

I pressed my lips together and nodded, then remembered he couldn't see me. "Yeah."

"So, let's do it. You need me."

"No." I lifted my chin. "I don't need you, actually. I think I have to do it on my own from now on. If you want a friend, go hang out with Ashley. I'm sure she'd be happy to kiss you and have it mean absolutely nothing." And then I hung up and tossed my phone aside. I deserved more than what he could give me, and I didn't need a pity practice from him.

I was wearing my new cleats and walking across the field to JV practice on Thursday when I felt someone fall into step beside me. No, there was someone on both sides of me.

I dragged my gaze off the ground and looked up. It was

Sara and Beth. One on either side. Trapping me. "What do you want?" I snapped.

"To apologize," Sara announced.

I shot her a disbelieving look. "Are you kidding?"

"Nope." She and Beth exchanged glances. "See, I've been sort of hanging out with Kirk this week."

I kicked at a tuft of grass and kept walking. "I noticed."

"He likes me."

"Great."

"And it's because of you."

I looked up at that. "What?"

Sara shrugged, looking sheepish. "He told me about your conversation at Pop's with him. How you told him I was actually cool, if he'd just look for it. Because of what you said, he noticed me. And because of what you told me about acting dumb around him, when he did start paying attention, I dropped the act." She smiled, her eyes bright with happiness. "So now, we're . . . kind of dating. And I owe you for it. So I love you and I'm sorry. Really. I've been a jerk." She slung her arm over my shoulder. "And the cool thing is, that when I started working hard this week on soccer to bust you, I realized how much I love the game. It's fun to sweat! So you got me the guy and helped me realize what I wanted. And I'm so sorry for how badly I treated you."

"I'm thrilled for you," I mumbled. Or I would be, if she weren't stealing all my dreams.

Her smile faltered. "What's wrong? Why aren't you happy for me? Do you want me to kiss your toes or something?"

Toe kissing wasn't going to cut it. "No, it's fine."

They both frowned at me.

"Are you still mad?" Sara asked. "I meant it when I said I was sorry. Since when do you hold a grudge?"

I shook my head as we approached the field for our last JV practice before tryouts happened tomorrow. "No, it's other stuff."

"Like Graham?" Beth asked.

I shot her a look. "What do you know about Graham? Did he say something to you?"

"No, but I noticed you guys weren't practicing this week. What's up?"

Coach Merrill blew her whistle for us to do a warm-up lap around the field, and we fell in together in the back.

Sara bumped me with her shoulder. "So? What's going on?"

I pressed my lips together and shook my head. "I don't want to talk about it." I actually did want to talk about it, but I was still too mad about their betrayal to tell them. I mean, yeah, she apologized, but it wasn't enough. I was still mad. So I sped up and left them behind, and I could hear them whispering behind me.

I didn't care.

After a few seconds, they caught up with me again. "So, we're going to stay and practice with you tonight," Sara announced.

I snorted. "It's Thursday night. Pop's night. You never stay late on Thursdays, especially now that you have a boyfriend."

"We're staying," Sara said firmly. "I've been hanging out with Coach Merrill and eavesdropping, and I know it's between you and Kathleen for the second spot. And I know what her weakness is, and I know what yours is. And I can help you fix it tonight."

I was completely unable to stop the hope from flaring in my chest. "Oh, come *on*."

She grabbed my arm and tugged me to a stop so I was facing her. "I'll stay here all night if that's what it takes to help you make varsity. I owe you."

I inspected her. She looked serious. "You're the number one spot?"

"Yeah, but if you don't make it, I'll drop out so you can have my spot." She put her hand over her heart. "I swear on the watery grave of my dead goldfish Herman that I'll drop out if I make it and you come in third."

That got my attention. To invoke Herman was way serious. "But I thought you just said that you realized you wanted varsity?"

"I do, but I owe you. I'll walk away if I need to. Herman Swear."

I stared at her, my throat getting tight. I could tell that Sara was totally serious about how much she wanted varsity, and she was willing to Herman Swear her spot over to me if it came down to that. I nodded my acceptance of her apology. "Thanks."

"So, am I forgiven?"

I nodded. "Only because of the Herman Swear."

Beth gave a small whoop of joy and threw her arms around both of us. "I'm going to miss you guys so much when you both make varsity!"

I hugged them both back, and Sara did too. "You guys are the best," I said. "Even if I did hate you earlier in the week."

"Ditto," Sara laughed.

Coach Merrill blew her whistle. "Girls! Aren't you supposed to be running?"

We giggled and started running again, hopelessly behind the rest of the team. And for the first time since Saturday, I felt better.

But I still couldn't keep myself from checking out

Graham's field after practice to see if he was there.

He wasn't. "Our" field was empty.

All week, I'd thought that he was still there, practicing. Hoping I'd show up.

But he wasn't. I'd cut him off, and he'd let me.

It was now officially over between us. Even as friends, it was no more.

And I felt like my heart was going to break.

13

*W*e practiced until almost eleven o'clock Thursday night. My mom came and brought us dinner, and then hung out while we practiced. By the time I went to bed, I was so unbearably tired that I almost didn't lie awake thinking about the tryouts and Graham and Sara and Kirk and everything else. Almost.

And then it was Friday.

The morning of the day of the tryouts.

And then it was Friday afternoon, and it was *time* for tryouts.

I walked out onto the field, flanked by Sara and Beth, my nerves in knots. The JV girls practice was going to be combined with the varsity girls practice, but Beth and her group were going to be separate.

Sara and I were going to be matched with a varsity girl. I scanned the fields as we approached. Kirk and Ross were sitting in the bleachers and they gave us a thumbs-up.

But no Graham.

I searched again, fighting against the disappointment. I'd been so certain he would come. This is what we'd been working for together. How could he not be here to support me?

But he wasn't there. He simply *wasn't there*.

"Who are you looking for?" Sara asked.

"No one."

"Duh, she's looking for Graham," Beth said. "What's up with you guys? You still haven't told us anything."

I shook my head and steeled myself against the wave of misery. "Today is about soccer." No way was I going to screw up tryouts because I was bumming about Graham. "The varsity coach is here."

Coach Young stood next to Coach Merrill, with a clipboard in her hand.

Suddenly I felt nauseated. I stopped where I was. "I can't do this."

"Yes, you can." Sara grabbed my arm and started dragging me toward the bench, but I twisted out of her reach, my hands shaking.

"No, I can't. What if I screw up?" I set my hands on my thighs and bent over, trying to catch my breath from my chest, which had suddenly gotten tight. I'd worked so hard for it, and now it was here. "I screwed up so badly at the last practice with them. This is my last chance."

"So, if you fail, you'll be on JV with me and we'll have fun," Beth said. "What's so bad about that?"

"It's just . . ." I closed my eyes and tried to breathe. They didn't understand. No one would understand how important this was.

I felt a hand on my back, then someone leaned next to me.

My heart leaped, and my eyes popped open. "Graham?"

But it was my mom. She squatted next to me and patted my shoulder. "You'll be great. You're good enough. You don't even have to play your best and you'll make it."

I stared at her, the tension in my body beginning to ease. "What if I can't play?"

She smiled. "You'll be fine." She held out her cell phone. "Someone wants to talk to you."

I grabbed the phone. "Graham?"

"Hey, Trisha," my dad said. "How you doing?"

"Dad?" I frowned. "Why are you calling me?"

"Because I couldn't make it there, but I wanted you to

know I was thinking of you. You'll do great."

I kicked a tuft of grass and took a deep breath. He was right. I could be great. "I can do this."

"You bet you can. How about dinner Sunday night?"

I lifted my head. "Really? Dinner with you and me?"

"Yep. To celebrate making varsity."

I grinned. "Okay." Coach Merrill blew her whistle. "I gotta go. Bye."

I hung up and handed the phone back to my mom, feeling better already. Sara slung her arm over my shoulder. "Okay, Trisha, here's the thing. Last time you screwed up because you were trying too hard. All you need to do is focus, like you do in practice. Think about the ball and the game, not about varsity or anything like that." She tapped her head. "Your problem is that you're too intense out there. I'm better because I relax and go with the flow and let myself succeed instead of forcing it."

I eyed her, rolling her advice over in my mind. It made sense. "Thanks."

"Let's go kick some butt, okay?" She gave me a smile that was all attitude.

Her expression fired me up. "You got it."

We strode up to the group of varsity girls, and when Coach Young assigned me to pair up with the same varsity chick as last time, the one who had dominated me, Sara leaned over and whispered: "You're as good as she is.

140

Believe it, and go with your instincts."

I thought of how much I'd practiced with Graham, and the late-night drilling session with Sara and Beth last night, and I knew it was true. I did believe it.

Two and a half hours later, I was sweaty, exhausted, and fired up beyond belief. Lisa, my varsity opponent, had dusted me a few times, but I'd beat her too. It was so unbelievably awesome to be up against such good players, and once I took Sara's advice and stopped worrying about it, I'd just let myself go, and I'd had a fantastic time.

Coach Young whistled us in, and I flopped next to Sara on the grass. She was drenched in sweat as well, and even had a grass stain on her shoulder. "How'd it go?" I asked.

She beamed at me. "Awesome."

Beth sat next to us, still looking almost as fresh as she had when we'd walked out onto the field. "Well, practice was totally boring without you two there," she announced. "If you both make varsity, I think I'm going to try out for the musical and bag sports. Soccer's really boring if you actually just play soccer, you know?"

Sara and I grinned at each other, and I realized that for the first time in forever, someone besides Graham actually got me too.

Coach Young blew her whistle. "First of all, I want to say thank you to the JV team for practicing with us today.

It's always great to see the up-and-coming talent."

The varsity girls politely clapped for us, and Sara, Beth, and I cheered loudly.

"So, as you all know, we have two open spots on varsity this year. I would like to welcome the following girls to the team: Sara Myers."

My gut tightened as Sara screamed and jumped to her feet, and the crowd burst out in cheers. I was happy for her. I really was, but I wanted it so badly as well.

"And the second player is . . ." She paused to confer with Coach Merrill, and I saw Coach Merrill's eyes go to me.

I sat up, my heart starting to race. It was me. They'd picked *me*.

Coach Young looked up from her notes. "The second player is Kathleen Hoffman."

Kathleen shrieked and the place cheered, and I stared numbly at the grass as my insides shriveled up. *I hadn't made it.*

Beth touched my arm, but I couldn't look at her.

Then Sara sat back down and leaned toward me. "Herman Swear, Trisha. My spot is yours."

But I shook my head and looked at her. "I don't want your spot. You earned it. Getting a spot that way, it would be like cheating."

She frowned. "You're sure?"

I nodded, and saw the relief in her eyes, and I knew

then that she really would have given up her spot.

But I couldn't take it. Not that way.

A varsity girl grabbed Sara's arm and congratulated her, and I clenched my fists. All I wanted to do was leave.

One of the coaches blew the whistle again, over the screams of all the girls. It took three more tries before people quieted down enough to hear what Coach Young was saying. I stared at the ground and wished this was over, barely listening to the yammering of the coach who was not going to be my coach. "Due to the talent of the JV squad, we decided to add a third roster spot. Trisha Perkins, welcome to varsity."

What? I jerked my head up as Beth shrieked next to me. Sara yelled and tackled me in a huge hug that knocked me onto my back. I grunted as I fell over, disbelief making me numb. "We both made it," Sara shouted. "You did it!"

"Oh, my God!" Beth dove on top of us, hugging us both. "I'm going to miss you guys so much! You're so awesome!"

Twisting to the side so I could see past Sara's embrace, I looked up at Coach Merrill, and she gave me the thumbs-up, and that's when it sank in. I'd made varsity.

I'd made varsity.

I jumped to my feet, screaming. "I made it! I made it!"

My friends screamed back and hugged me, and we all yelled and danced. And then my mom came over and we all hugged her, and then we called my dad, and I could tell he was happy, and I realized Graham had been so right about him—

Graham.

After I hung up with my dad, I held the phone in my hand. My mom was talking to Coach Young to find out the hours of practice, and when games were. I watched Sara get a hug from Kirk, and I envied Beth as she and Ross bent their heads together in deep conversation.

Graham might not have come today, and I might not be talking to him, but he was part of the reason I'd made the team. He deserved to know. I was pretty sure he'd be psyched.

So I dialed his number from memory, hoping he would answer the phone, at the same time I hoped he wouldn't.

He didn't.

It went to voice mail, and I smiled at the sound of his voice. He still made me feel good. "Graham, this is Trisha. I just wanted to let you know . . ."

"Trisha!" Sara was suddenly next to me. "We're going to Pop's to celebrate. You're coming, right?"

I braced against my instinct to refuse, and I nodded. "Of course I am. Wouldn't miss it."

"Cool." She kissed my cheek, then ran back to Kirk and Beth and Ross. "She's coming."

"So, anyway, Graham," I continued, "tryouts are over

and I made varsity." I felt a smile break over my face. "Did you hear me? I made varsity!" I shouted the last bit, still too excited to contain myself. "And it was partly because of our practices, so thanks. Gotta go!" Then I shut the phone, gave it to my mom, and ran after my friends into the gym.

Who cared if Graham had blown me off? I'd proved I could do it on my own and I wasn't going to let him ruin my celebration. I didn't need him. I was a varsity soccer player now!

"Here's to Sara and Trisha, varsity soccer players." Beth raised her root beer. "Yay!"

We all toasted by tapping our red plastic cups against one another's. I grinned at my friends, not even caring that I was there with two couples. I'd made varsity! Soccer was what mattered. Not guys! Not dating. And certainly not Graham.

Kirk had his arm over Sara's shoulder, and even though Ross and Beth weren't near to that stage, they were sitting on the same side of the booth, almost touching shoulders, so they were on their way.

The cashier announced our number for our pizza. Kirk jumped up. "My treat tonight. I'll get it."

"I'll help." Ross slid out of the booth, and the guys headed up to the counter for our meal.

They weren't dating me, but if they wanted to buy my

celebratory dinner, I wasn't going to stop them. I grinned at Beth and Sara. "This is the greatest night. I never thought I had a chance, not after that horrible practice with varsity a couple of weeks ago."

Sara cocked her head. "Last night when we were drilling, I couldn't believe how much better you'd gotten. That practice time with Graham really helped, huh?"

I shrugged and suddenly felt deflated. "Sure."

She studied me. "What happened with him, anyway? All of a sudden, it's like he's disappeared off the planet."

Beth moved her drink out of the way so she could move closer to me. "Yeah. What happened?"

I fiddled with my napkin, shredding it into little pieces. "He's a dork." I shrugged. "I decided to blow him off. No biggie."

Beth cocked her head. "Why is he a dork?"

"Because he thinks he can kiss me whenever he wants and have it not mean anything."

Two sets of eyebrows went up and their jaws dropped. "He kissed you?"

"Yeah."

"*On the lips?*" Sara asked, her eyes glittering. "Was it nice?"

"Yeah, on the lips." I felt my cheeks get hot. "And yeah, really nice."

"So, what's the problem?" Sara sounded shocked. "Why

did you blow him off? You like him, he kisses you and it's great, and you ditch him? Why?"

I realized my napkin was fully shredded, so I pulled the dispenser toward me and tugged another one free and started working on that one. "He did it to show me that we were just friends, and—"

Sara shook her head. "No, no, you have *got* to start from the beginning."

I looked into the faces of my friends, realized how much I'd missed having them to talk to, and suddenly the whole story spilled out. The *whole* thing.

When I finished, they were both smirking.

I scowled at them. "What's so funny? He blew me away with the best kiss in the world, and then ruined it by saying it meant nothing. How is that funny?" I saw Kirk and Ross finish paying for the pizzas and start to head back to the table. "Never mind. We'll talk about it later."

Sara chuckled. "It's funny because you and Graham are both such idiots."

"Me? How am I an idiot?"

The boys arrived with the pizza and I leaned back in my seat and gave Beth and Sara the "I don't want to talk about it in front of them" look.

Sara nodded, then looked up at Kirk as he slid in next to her. "So, if a guy kissed a girl on the lips, like a really good kiss, would you believe him if he said he did it to prove he didn't like her?"

"Sara!" I kicked her under the table, missed, and slammed my toe into the leg, sending pain shooting up my foot.

Kirk snorted. "No way. If he claimed that's why he kissed her, he's lying. It's just an excuse to cover up the real reason he kissed her."

"Sara, I swear I will kill you if you don't shut up."

Kirk looked at me as he tugged a slice of pizza free. "Why? Did Graham feed you that line after he kissed you or something?"

I balled up the napkin and hurled it at him. He didn't even flinch when it bounced off his forehead. "Shut up," I growled.

Kirk grinned and Sara gave me a smug look. "He kissed you because he wanted to, then had to make up a reason afterward," Sara said.

"No way." I gave up trying to get them to abandon the conversation. "Afterward, I hinted that I liked the kiss and he totally panicked! If he liked me, he wouldn't have panicked when he thought I liked him."

"Not necessarily," Ross said.

We all looked at him in surprise. I didn't realize the guy actually spoke in public.

He shrugged. "He might have panicked because he liked you."

Beth nodded. "Totally! I mean, you both were totally anti-dating, right? And then you start to like him and you panic. And he starts to like you but figures it's okay because you don't like him, then he realizes you like him and he isn't prepared for that. So he panics and makes up that stupid line about kissing you to prove he doesn't like you."

"That makes no sense." I resumed my napkin shredding with even more force.

"Guys make no sense," Sara agreed. She beamed at Kirk. "Even you."

He grinned back. "Girls make even less sense."

"No way. It's all boys."

I rolled my eyes as the table descended into a totally annoying and cute argument between couples about which gender made less sense. I grabbed a paper plate and pulled two slices of Meat Lover's Deluxe onto my plate, letting it wash thoughts of Graham out of my head.

He was history and I was moving on.

I picked up my pizza and blew on the end to cool it off before I took a bite, almost chuckling when I thought of how I'd spilled pizza onto Graham's shoe. I tested the cheese with my finger to make sure it wasn't going to burn the roof of my mouth off, then took a bite.

A boot landed with a thunk in front of me, right on the edge of the table. "Need this?"

I looked up to see Graham standing there, his foot up

on the table, grinning at me. I was vaguely aware of the rest of the table falling silent. I swallowed my bite. "No, I'm good. I learned my lesson."

"You sure?"

After a second, I took a pepperoni off my slice and set it on his toe. "Thanks. I was looking for a place to stash that."

He grinned, took the pepperoni, and popped it in his mouth. "So, I got your message. Congratulations on varsity. That's awesome."

I couldn't help but smile. "Thanks. I was totally psyched."

He nodded. "I knew you could do it."

"Yeah, well, I had my doubts, but it worked out." I shrugged, suddenly not quite sure what to say. "So, um, how have you been?"

His gaze flicked to the rest of the table, all of whom were listening intently, then back to me. "Okay. You?"

I refused to think about how cute he looked in his oversize plaid shirt hanging out of his jeans, with the cuffs rolled up, or how much I missed being with him. So I put on a big, fake grin. "I just made varsity, so I'm awesome."

"Right." He sort of shifted his weight and shoved his hands in his pockets, moving his gaze to the gang again. "So, um, it looks like you're busy, so I'll just hit the road."

He hesitated and looked right at me.

What? What was that look for? "Okay, thanks for stopping by."

He nodded a greeting at the rest of the table, then started to turn away, then turned back. "Congratulations again, Trisha. I'm really psyched for you."

Then, before I could answer, he turned around and walked out.

The door had just shut behind him when Sara whacked me on the side of the head with my stack of napkins. "Idiot! Why are you still sitting here?"

I batted the napkins away. "What are you talking about?"

"Graham!" She whacked me again. "He came here tonight looking for you, and you totally let him go!"

"Hey!" I ducked as the napkin assault came back for a third try. "How would he know I was here? I'm sure he just ran into me."

"Weren't you on the phone with him when I came up and told you we were going to Pop's?" Sara didn't wait for my answer. She kicked me under the table. "He's getting away! Go after him!"

"So he can reject me again?" I jerked my throbbing shin out of her reach, then sat back and folded my arms. "Forget it."

"Reject you? He came here *for* you," Beth said. She looked at Kirk. "Didn't he?"

"Looks that way to me," Kirk said. "But you didn't invite him to hang with us, and you said you were excellent even though he wasn't around. If I were him, I'd take off too."

"But . . ."

Beth grabbed the napkins from Sara and whacked me on the head. "Go after him!"

"But . . ."

Ross nodded. "I think they're right. If I liked a girl, and if she gave me your attitude, I'd leave too."

Beth smiled at him. "I would never have given you the reaction Trish gave Graham."

He grinned back. "That's why I'm sitting here."

I stared at them, the two shyest people on the planet. They'd actually, somehow, figured out that they liked each other. Were they right? Should I go? Was there some subliminal boy/girl dating language that had just totally gone over my head?

They all turned and looked at me, then shouted in unison, "Go!"

"I'm going!" My heart suddenly racing, I slipped out of the booth, sprinted across the restaurant, ducking around kids, and flew out into the street. No Graham.

I looked both ways, looked down the street.

No Graham.

Crud! I'd missed him!

Then I thought of him, and I knew where he was.

Biting my lip in nervous anticipation, I started walking down the street toward the ice-cream shop, then I broke into a jog, and by the time I reached it, I was in a dead sprint. I skidded to a stop out front. The place was packed with people, and our bench was taken by a mom and her three kids.

He had to be here. I knew he had to be.

I hauled open the door, then jumped back in surprise as Graham nearly fell into me, a massive chocolate-dipped waffle cone in his hand. "Graham!" I jumped back as the ice cream flew out of his cone and onto my shirt. The top scoop landed with a thud and I caught it in my palm as it slid down my shirt.

I lifted my hand up, chocolate ice cream dripping from between my fingers. "How did you know I wanted a bite? You're so nice." I took a slurpy mouthful, and was rewarded with a half smile from him.

He held out his cone without a word, and I dumped the ice cream back into it, then started licking the ice cream off my hand.

He tossed me a napkin. "Aren't you missing out on

your celebration?" He started walking down the street.

My friends were right. He *was* miffed that I hadn't invited him to join us. "Yeah, but . . ." Could I really do this? Could I really tell him I liked him?

"But what?" He didn't look at me, but I heard the expectant tone in his voice.

So I said it. "I just thought it would be appropriate to celebrate with you, since you helped me get there."

He slanted a glance at me. "Really?"

"Really." I took a deep breath, then chickened out. I just couldn't take that look on his face again, the one where he acted like I had rabies or something.

We walked in silence for a few minutes, and I realized we were heading in the direction of my house. He handed me his cone without a word, and I took a bite. "Thanks."

He nodded.

And still we said nothing.

So . . . what now?

He stopped suddenly and turned toward me. "Did you like it when I kissed you?"

I blinked. "Um . . ." What was the right answer? What was he looking for?

He scowled and spun away. "Never mind," he muttered. "Forget I asked."

"No!" I ran after him, grabbed his arm, and made him

stop. "Yes, I liked it. I liked it a lot. That's why I couldn't take hanging out with you, because that's all I could think about whenever I saw you, but you weren't thinking about it at all, and I felt so awkward and—"

"Wrong."

I frowned. "What?"

"You're wrong." He was looking at me intently, his eyes dark and intense in the shadows from the streetlight. "I was thinking about it. All the time."

Suddenly, I had trouble swallowing. "You were?"

He nodded. "See, the thing is, I liked it too."

I felt like someone had just dropped a brick on my head. "You . . . did?"

"Took me a while to figure it out, though. What I thought. What you thought." He held out his cone. "Here."

Ice cream? I didn't want ice cream right now! But I took it when he practically shoved it in my hand.

Then I forgot about the ice cream when he put his hands on either side of my face and leaned toward me, his gaze intent on mine. His hands were warm, and he gently rubbed his thumbs against my cheeks, like he was waiting to see if I was going to tell him to back off. When I didn't, he got this little smile on his face, and then he bent down and kissed me, and it was even better than before. Softer, slower, and perfect, making little chills rush down my arms. He tasted like chocolate, like warm, melted chocolate.

He broke the kiss and pulled back slightly. "So, that was a test."

I blinked, trying to remember my name and how to breathe. "What?"

"I had to see if my theory still stood. You know, that a guy and a girl can kiss on the lips and still be just friends."

"*What?*" I stepped back, clutching his ice cream. "We're back to that again? Are you *kidding?*"

He took my hand before I could get out of reach. "And my conclusion is that maybe other people can kiss and have it mean nothing, but we can't."

I stopped trying to get away. "What are you saying?" I had to know for sure.

"I'm saying . . ." He tugged gently on my hand and I let him pull me closer. "I'm saying that I like you. Like, *like.*"

"Are you sure? I mean, you kinda freaked that day on the soccer field."

"Well, the thing is, I missed you this week. I'd gotten used to hanging out with you and when I couldn't any-more . . . it bummed me out." He tugged on my ponytail, and this time it didn't make me think that we were only friends. It made me think that I liked him, and I liked being with him. "So?"

I grinned at him, my happiness nearly bubbling out of my head. "So what?"

He groaned. "Cut me some slack here, Trisha. I'm not exactly used to telling girls I like them, you know? Are you in or not?"

I laughed, unable to keep it inside any longer. "Graham, you're a total idiot if you can't figure out that I like you too."

"Really?" He got this huge smile on his face.

"Swear."

He slipped his hands around my waist and pulled me against him, tossing the ice cream cone over his shoulder. It landed with a splat on the sidewalk. "So, does that mean I have a varsity girlfriend?"

I giggled like a total girl and linked my hands behind his neck. "Yeah, I guess it does."

"Sweet." Then he bent his head, and I stood up on my tiptoes and we met in the middle.

And it was perfect.

*If you liked this,
you'll fall for*

Love at First Click

by Eliabeth Chandler

School was buzzing Thursday and Friday. Flynn and Nicole. Breeze and Jared. Who would have guessed?

Perhaps I should have felt worse for Flynn and Breeze, both of them finding themselves unexpectedly dumped. But I had been through so many breakups with Breeze—and listened to her brokenhearted boyfriends, who, after all that time hanging out in our family room, mistook me for their sister—I just couldn't get all worked up about it. Besides, the cool and the gorgeous usually survive. And there were a million girls feeling sympathetic toward Flynn. I exaggerate, there were only six to eight at any one time clustered around him.

1

"What *was* Nicole thinking?" Paige asked, shaking her head.

Of course, it was terribly tacky to dump a guy four days after a season-ending injury, an injury over which an entire stadium had held its breath. But I knew how Nicole's mind worked.

She ran in the same ultracool circles that Breeze did, and it was important for her that she not only liked the guy she dated, but that he gave her status. He was expected to provide a ticket to events that were cool to be seen at. She was smart enough to know that, while Flynn was hero of the moment, with each new football game, his rating would drop, at least as compared to the cool ratings of other players. In a sense, both Coach Siefert and she were scanning the team to see who would replace Flynn. Unlike Coach, she had other leagues to consider. Word flew fast that she had attended the drama group tryouts Thursday afternoon. *Perhaps*, I thought, *she was as sick of the football schedule as Breeze.*

Friday's football game was at a school about twenty minutes away from Saylor Mill. Kids traveled in caravans, and Gabriel, Jenny, and I hitched a ride with Kathleen.

Breeze asked if she could come with us that night. We squeezed together and let her sit quietly, staring out the window. Since my sister could have driven herself, I figured she was really hurting. Knowing the coaches of other teams were not as fanatical about rules as Siefert, I made an offer. "Would you like to hang with me on the sidelines?" I asked. "I've got an extra camera you can wear around your neck."

For a moment her eyes went misty. "You're my best sister!"

"Your only," I reminded her.

She nodded. "But I'm cool. I can deal with this. I guess I'll find out who my real friends are," she added, and headed for the stands in an outfit that would draw guys like flies to honey. Oh, yeah, she could deal with this.

In the course of the game, it looked as if a junior named Gavin Thompson might replace Flynn, especially after he snagged a pass, shook off two defenders, and ran in for a touchdown. Too bad he fumbled on the next offensive effort, and the other team recovered it and ran it in for a score. Really too bad, because we lost to a team we should have beaten.

After the fumble, Flynn went over and stood next to Gavin—didn't say anything, just stood next to him. It was the only way one player could support another who'd made a terrible mistake: just be there for him and say through your actions, *that's okay, we're in this together*. I found myself admiring Flynn for doing that, especially when nobody else did.

As agreed earlier, those of us who came with Kathleen

gathered at her car fifteen minutes after the game ended. Breeze sent a message through Jenny that she had found another ride home. Kathleen made the rounds, dropping us off at our front doors, and I was the last one.

Entering our house, standing in the entrance to the family room, I could see that a light was on in the kitchen. I knew Dad went to bed early after long projects like his last. "Hi, Breeze," I called in to my sister.

"Hey, Hayley," she called back.

"That game sure was the pits," I said, setting down my camera bag and pack. "We could have done better if Flynn had played one-armed, and if he'd left his head and helmet on the bench!"

Breeze didn't reply, but a round of deep laughter came from the kitchen. Her ride home.

"I guess you're hungry," Breeze called out to me.

"Have I ever come back from watching beefy guys beat each other up and not wanted something from the deli drawer?"

Another deep laugh.

Breeze knew I liked to eat after games. I figured that if she had wanted privacy, she would have taken her "ride home" to the back deck.

"I have a zillion pictures to download," I said, entering the kitchen. "I'm just going to make a sandwich to—to,

4

uh, take, uh . . . to my room."

"Hello." Flynn's voice was as warm as his smile. He and Breeze were sitting on the barstools along one side of our center island. His slate-colored eyes gazed at me with friendly curiosity.

"Hi."

"This is my sister, Hayley," Breeze said.

"Really? I wouldn't have guessed." He looked from me to Breeze. "I don't think I even knew you had a sister."

"We're twins," I told him.

He glanced at me with surprise. I shouldn't have said it, but he wasn't the first guy who found it amazing that Breeze and I came from the same gene pool.

"Uh, fraternal?" he replied uncertainly, and Breeze laughed. She was using her girly, tinkling laugh.

"Just kidding," I told him, and turned my back, glad to have a refrigerator to open and stare into. *Why did she have to choose him?* I thought. Of course, both of them had just been jilted, so it was natural enough that they'd find each other. Had she flirted first? Maybe he had. Why should I care?

"Hayley is a sophomore," Breeze told Flynn.

"Do you go to Saylor Mill?" he asked.

I turned toward him holding a bag of meat and the mayo jar, with perhaps not the friendliest look on my

5

face. Apparently he had never noticed me on the sidelines. I wondered if he would have recognized Gabriel. *He'd have to*, I thought, *Gabriel did interviews.* And then again, if your ego is the size of Saturn . . .

"I guess so," he said, "if you just came from the game."

I took out a plate and an evil-looking knife (we'd forgotten to turn the dishwasher on, so our everyday silverware was dirty). Breeze, equally unwilling to hand wash something, had gotten two good china bowls out of the dining room corner cupboard.

"Chocolate swirl or butter pecan?" she asked Flynn, as she slipped off her stool and opened the freezer.

"Whatever is open," he said, then turned to me. "Saylor is a huge school."

"Yes, it is."

"And, of course, the way the class schedules are, people from different years don't cross over in the hallway that much."

"If ever," I said, not because I wanted to get him off the hook, but because I wanted to end a miserable conversation that proved he had never even *slightly* noticed me, despite the fact that I was the only one who photographed the team.

"Of course, Hayley does all the photo coverage for the football team," Breeze told him.

"She does?"

I glanced up from the meat I was piling onto my slab of bread.

"You do?" At least he was polite enough to turn pink.

I wiped my hands on a dish towel, picked up my own digital, which I had left on the kitchen counter, and held it up in front of my face. "Now do I look familiar?"

His color deepened.

"Don't worry about it," I said, setting down the camera. "At practice, Coach is always telling you to focus. He'd be thrilled to know how well you're listening."

Flynn looked at me long and thoughtfully, and now I could feel myself turning pink. I flattened my roast beef with a second piece of bread and sliced the sandwich with one stroke of the evil-looking knife.

"About two weeks ago," Flynn said, "I ran over a photographer on the sidelines."

"You didn't tell me that!" Breeze exclaimed to me. Then she added, "*That's* where you got that big bruise on your butt. It was amazing, Flynn, all different shades of purple, like a bouquet of pansies."

"Thank you for that detail, Breeze," I said, and turned to put away the meat and mayo. I couldn't wait to get out of there.

But as I picked up my sandwich, Flynn ducked his head, trying to catch my eye and make me look at him. It was impossible to look away. Maybe that was how he beat his opponents—he hypnotized them with his gorgeous eyes.

"I hope you're okay," he said.

"Yes, I have some natural padding there."

He held on to my eyes. "I, uh, I'm really sorry."

I knew from his tone he was apologizing not only for tossing me on my rump, but for never noticing me. Now my ego was bruised more than my butt had ever been.

"Not a problem," I told him, and got out of the kitchen as fast as I could.

Five minutes later, I was staring at photos on my computer screen and sipping the flat Coke I had found in my room—I'd been in too big a hurry to remember to grab a drink. I couldn't figure out why it bothered me so much that Flynn Delancy was in our kitchen. Maybe it was because his presence there broke the sacred rules of a camera crush.

A camera crush isn't much different from any kind of secret crush. Lots of people have had the experience of that one face that captures your attention from across a crowded room—in my case, it was across a crowded football field and on the other side of a telephoto lens. Whatever. The rules of having a secret crush were that you tingled a little when you saw that face, you imagined things about the person who belonged to the face—things that probably had nothing to do with who the person really was—and you never, *ever* crossed the distance between you and that person. It would ruin the dream! It would blow away the fantasy!

Unfortunately, when a secret crush begins eating stuff out of your refrigerator, he becomes a little too real.

I had just finished my flat soda when Breeze knocked on my door.

"Come in."

She stood for several minutes, watching over my shoulder as I clicked on the four game photos that I thought were my best.

"You're really good at what you do, Hayley."

"Thanks. This new camera the school bought really helps. It writes incredibly fast to the disk."

"Mmm," she said, already losing interest. Then she laughed and threw herself across my bed. "What *was* I thinking? What *was* I ever thinking?"

I clicked on another photo and rotated it on my screen. "You have to make it easier for me to guess. What were you thinking *when*?"

"When I dated Jared."

"Oh." I sighed. "Probably the same thing you thought when you dated all the other guys."

"But this time things are different," Breeze said. "He's gorgeous, isn't he?"

"Who?" I asked. Like I didn't know!

"Flynn. Flynn Delancy."

"Yeah, he's gorgeous."

She pulled herself up on her elbow. "He's not like any guy I've dated."

I'd heard those words before.

"He's got a great body. Eyes to die for. A sense of humor."

"A high rating in the School of Cool," I added.

"All in one package," Breeze said, leaping up from the bed and spinning around. I had to laugh. If this had been a musical, she would have broken into song.

"Did you ask him for a ride?"

"No," Breeze replied. "No no no! Flynn asked me. He found me during halftime, actually came looking for me! It's nice to be *appreciated*."

She looked over my shoulder again. "Those are photos from tonight's game," she said, sounding disappointed.

"Well, yeah."

"Do you have some from other games on this computer?"

"Sure."

"Print me out some pictures of Flynn," she said, leaning down to give me a hug from behind. "You're my best sister!"

She danced out the door, and I continued to work on the photos I had just taken, though not as happily as before.